Who's
Rock Hard?

Alex A Hunter

A novel

D&S Cooper Books

Who's Rock Hard?

First published by D&S Cooper Books in 2015, Maryborough Qld, Australia

Cover photo by Bella Dee Photography

(Make-up & hair artistry by Shantel May)

ISBN 978-0-9924049-9-4

Chapter One

Her lips twitched, threatening to erupt into a full blown smile as she made her escape. *Nearly there.*

She'd done it. She'd made her break. Her heart pounded as a rush of blood pumped through her body. Her eyes fixed ahead, concentration unwavering. The urge to run tugged at her insides. But she fought it. She needed to be calm, *blend in.*

She stole a glance ahead. *Not long now.* She sensed it coming. Every fibre, every pore on her skin, burned hot with need. Her legs were like jelly as a shot of excitement ripped through her, every step bringing her closer to – *freedom!*

She'd endured the past two hours of torture. Survived it – and now it was over. *Almost.*

Sharp bursts of applause exploded in the air behind her, drowning out the soft click of her evening heels. She kept moving, barely flinching, as she slipped past the last of the tables, marking the end of the room. She heard her own heartbeat, so loud she thought it would burst against her ribcage.

She let a hand stray to the top of a chair, steadying her stride. Her fingers brushing over the cool, white satin cover – fingertips catching in the big looped bow. Then she was out of the room. *Finally.*

She hit a cool rush of air now unencumbered by the harsh, forced mix of manufactured scents and eau de toilettes of the audience she'd left behind. She drew in a deep breath, allowing the air's icy freshness to fill her lungs. Rejuvenated, she hastened her step. She wasn't safe yet.

She had bided her time for the best part of the evening, sitting at the most brain numbing conference she'd ever attended. She'd swapped all the right small talk and flashed all the right smiles. Then in the bustle of a change of speaker, she'd seen her chance and slipped away from her table.

Now she was out.

She crossed the wide expanse of the conference centre foyer, and headed towards the winding staircase that led to the mezzanine level – *and would take her to safety.* She made it to the staircase unseen, then with gentle taps of her shoes, she made her way up the large, stone steps.

She glanced back. She could see the lectern in the middle of the stage in front of the tables. She knew she'd risked the next speaker, witnessing her escape – *collateral damage.* She had to get out of there.

A small, string quartet sat just off the stage – its job to fill in the gaps between speakers. She heard the soft remnants of its latest rich harmony fall away to allow the next speaker to begin.

At the top of the staircase, she turned right and cut

through a lounged seating area, and headed towards a narrow hallway. Then she saw it – *her safe haven.* A wave of relief swept over her and her heartbeat slowed back to a more comfortable rhythm.

She felt her heels sink into the plush carpet. Then she let out the smile she'd been holding at bay. The carpet would muffle any noise from her shoes. *Not far now.*

She stepped up the pace, checking out the long mezzanine space as she walked through it. She knew this level was also used for functions – but not today. Today it was a ghost town – dark, quiet, closed for business. A spark of happiness flickered inside her at the sight of the deserted area, and she let out a breath of relief. *Nobody here.*

A renewed surge of energy pushed her along. Her stride long and swift, sent the silky fabric of her evening gown billowing up behind her. Its soft touch shimmied across her ankles. She closed her eyes for a second, her body started to relax. *Peace.*

The speaker's voice boomed an introduction through the microphone, shaking her from her momentary trance. If she risked a glance over the balcony, she'd be able to see the guests on the ground floor below. All dressed to the nines – all seated at perfect tables, decorated with perfect tablecloths, overstuffed centrepieces, and all the usual trappings of fine etiquette.

She'd attended too many of these functions – and she was bored out of her mind. She did on occasion enjoy the extravagant displays. But most of the time she just felt trapped, like an animal, doomed to suffer the stifling and suffocating rhetoric.

She mapped a wide path from the balcony, its generous height keeping her hidden from view. Her eyes riveted ahead, she focused on her mission – she needed to stay invisible as she headed towards her secret little room. She imagined it now – that little room that held all manner of luxuries – that secret little room where she could pause from the forced gaieties below and breathe. *Just breathe.*

She saw the white, wooden door up ahead. A few more steps and she'd be there. She read the glossy plaque on the door – "The Powder Room" – and smiled.

Thank God.

She delighted in the thought of stealing a few minutes to herself before the next half of the evening commenced. The next set of speeches was scheduled to include a question and answer time with the obligatory guest of honour. She knew she couldn't miss that – because *she* was the guest of honour.

She mused to herself about how clever she'd been – but distracted by her own thoughts, she'd missed one very important fact. That she was being watched – by a pair of intently curious, dark eyes.

A movement caught in her periphery. She glanced over, a shiver ran down her spine. Then she saw – *a man.*

Damn. Did her heart just skip a beat? Did he see her?

She snatched a second glance – tall, intolerably suave in a black tuxedo. *Damn. Hot. Did she stop breathing?*

But if her insides were churning, she didn't let it

show. She let her eyes lock onto the stranger's – for only a second. But a measly second was all it took. Her awareness of anything else around her vaulted into oblivion, and in that altered microcosm of time, a fire beat through her body like a crackling bushfire burning up everything in its path, yielding to no attempt to extinguish it.

But while the flash fire burned, she hid its flames. If her legs felt weak, she didn't stumble.

Did he feel that too?

She snapped her eyes from the stranger's, keeping her pace until she reached her destination. With a steady hand belying the chaos inside her, she reached out and lightly shoved the smooth, wooden panel on the powder room door.

She stepped inside, standing nearly to attention – alert – until she heard the soft thud of the door as it drew back closed behind her. She breathed out a heavy breath – s*afe again.*

On the other side of the door, the tall man in the black tuxedo approached.

He raised a hand and pushed against the same wooden door that he had seen the woman in the gold dress enter through only moments earlier.

***

"Katherine!" a female voice called out.

Katherine ignored it. Her focus shot back to her book, trying to pick up her place, as she mumbled. "A man in a tuxedo – a stranger? Powder room…."

"Katherine Wilkins! I need you down here for a minute!" Her housemate insisted.

Her eyes darted to her bedroom door then back to her book. She knew she was getting to a 'good bit'.

"Katherine!"

"Ok ok. I'm coming already." She plonked the book down, marked the page by leaving it open and upside down on her bed. The woman in the gold dress and the man in the tuxedo would just have to wait.

She smoothed out the wrinkles of her work skirt – she hadn't bothered to change. She'd barely made it to her room before ripping the paper bag off of her new book. She'd picked it up at the newsagents near the bus stop in the city. It was her Friday night treat, but she hadn't dared to open it until she'd made it home. It was one of 'those' books. She made a mental note to buy an electronic reading tablet so she could buy books online and read them in secret.

She stopped at the top of the stairs of their rented townhouse. "What's the big emergency Sal?"

No answer.

She huffed. Then scooted downstairs, but she'd only made it half way down when her eyes lit up at the sight of her housemate holding a massive bouquet of flowers, ribbons dangling.

"Wow. Who are they for?" She eyed off the brightly coloured blooms.

"Who do you think genius?" Sally handed them to her. "They were just delivered."

Katherine took in the sweet scent of the sunset coloured roses. "Wow. They're so pretty."

"Why so surprised?"

She shrugged. "I guess I'm just not used to getting flowers."

"Really?"

"Really."

She expected Sally would have been the more likely recipient, with her long, peroxide blonde hair, and ample bosom – she usually got all the male attention. Since she'd known Sally, Katherine had made peace with being 'the one with Sally' or 'Sal's friend'. *The quiet one with the brown hair and mousy features.* Yep, she was happy to just blend with the wallpaper.

"Who are they from?" Sally's smirk belied her attempt at innocence. "Quick read the card."

"As if you haven't already." She smiled and picked out the delicate card nestled between two flowers.

"Thank you for a lovely evening. Steven."

"Hmm…." Sally wiggled her eyebrows. "A lovely evening hey?"

"It was just dinner." But her bright smile hinted at the excitement that fluttered inside her, as she recalled her date with Steven. "He was a perfect gentleman."

"Uh-huh." Her friend's eyes narrowed. "Kat, you are a such a goody-two-shoes."

"What do you mean?"

"Men aren't gentleman." She wagged a finger. "And they are definitely not perfect."

Katherine inhaled a deep breath over the top of the flowers, delighting in the delicious aroma. "Well maybe you just haven't been hanging out with the right men."

"Maybe." She rolled her eyes at the thought of her own misshapen choice of men. "But I still reckon you need to get your nose out of those romance books of yours and go out and find a real man."

"Steven's a real man." *Wasn't he? Was her experience*

with men so limited?

Sally put a hand on her friend's shoulder. "Kat, honey." She paused for effect. "He's pretending. Men only behave like gentlemen when they want something."

She let her words hover. Then cocked her head to bring home her point. "They all pretend – when they want to impress you."

"I'm sure not all men are like that."

Sal sucked her lips in tight, then let them out with a pop. "Sure they are honey."

Katherine plucked a single rose out of the bouquet and ceremoniously handed it to her cynical pal. "Well, we are just going to have to disagree on that now aren't we?"

***

Katherine nestled back into the pillows on her bed, picked up her book, and quickly skimmed to find where she'd left off.

A tingle ran down her spine. She felt the delicious excitement of what was about to come in the story, and now with her delivery of flowers positioned beside her on the bedside table, she smiled as her heart beat a little faster with naughty anticipation.

If only Sal really knew. She started reading again.

'She stood statue still, and held her breath, until she heard the door to the powder room close behind her.

Alone. She flushed hot, nerve endings sizzling with excitement and relief. *Who was that man?*

She realised he'd probably watched her entire

journey from the top of the staircase – possibly even earlier. A rush of embarrassment pricked at her skin.

She touched a hand to her cheek and felt the heat he'd caused. She was shocked at her own reaction. Thoughts of the man outside sent ripples of pleasure through her body – he was hot and sexy as hell. *What a reaction.* This never happened to her.

But who was he? She stepped further into the room and tried to remember what she'd come in here for – but she was uncontrollably distracted.

Concierge? Guest? She didn't remember seeing him at the tables. *Bartender?* Hell, he could be the window washer for all she cared. He looked like Christmas. *One great big package to….*

She shook her head, snapped herself out of it. *What are you doing? Get a grip!* She hosed herself down with thoughts of professionalism and good social graces. She came here for a reason.

Two more steps forward and she was in front of a glossy, cream benchtop that sat directly under softly lit mirrors spaced along the wall. She set her small purse down and tried to focus on the sumptuous yet delicate features of the powder room.

But those eyes. Those dark, broody eyes. He had looked inside her soul, setting alight a cocktail of primal instinct and sexual hunger. She hardly recognised herself. *This wasn't her.*

She shook away the destructive thoughts that threatened to shake her resolve. She had a speech to deliver soon…very soon.

She inhaled several deliberate breaths, and patted her cheeks as they cooled. It seemed to work. She felt her heartbeat return to normal, and her surroundings came back into focus. Fresh bouquets of vibrant flowers sprouted from hand painted vases. They adorned each end of the benchtop. She closed her eyes and breathed in the soft, soothing perfume.

Then she heard a sound behind her. A bolt of fear shot through her. She caught her breath and spun around. *The door was opening. Someone was coming.*

She stood as still as she dared, willing her heartbeat to quiet. She looked up into the face of the man that entered.

It was him!

He didn't speak. He advanced into the room with predatory ease, then let the door close behind him.

A surge of shock pulsed through her – paralysing her. *What was he doing in here? In her safe haven. A woman's safe haven.* She looked up into his eyes – searched them. But they gave her nothing – each a black pit suspended over an abyss.

He moved a step closer, his eyes remained fixed on hers.

A rush of emotions coursed through her body. But somehow fear was no longer one of them.

He stepped aside, allowing her access to the door – if that's what she wanted.

Her left foot extended, her ankle exposed. But she pulled it back, placing it firmly back on the floor.

He waited.

Her heart pounded. She glanced at the door. *Why wasn't she leaving?*

Then she let her eyes trail back to his. Her heart beat an intolerable rhythm. She saw the need burning in his eyes – an unsatisfied, voracious need. A warning rippled through her, but she ignored it. She knew what he wanted – and to her own inconceivable belief, she realised – *she wanted it too.*

The smouldering ash fire burst to life inside her. Her heart hammered. Then she did the unthinkable. Betrayed by her own body…she took a step towards him.

She was weak to the invisible force that moved her body – powerless to resist. She didn't want to resist. Didn't want to move away. *How long had it been since she'd felt a man's touch?*

With silent understanding between them, she advanced further towards him.'

Katherine leaned the book against a pillow. Still in her work clothes, minus her shoes, she'd remained tucked up on her bed devouring the words on each page like a starving animal. Her legs, still clad in her work stockings, began to ache.

A shower, pyjamas, bed and back to her book – because she was getting to the good bit now and she wanted to savour every second.

Chapter Two

In a small town, three hours' drive north of Brisbane city, Max Martin stumbled through the solid timber front door of his modest, brick house.

He caught the steel cap of his suede work boots on the screen door tracking and tumbled forward, almost landing on the floor. Of course the line of empty beer bottles he'd drained after work – and left behind at the RSL – didn't help.

He laughed at his own clumsiness. *Hilarious.*

"Jenna!" He called out.

A petite, blonde woman, just as hilarious as Max snorted a response. "What?" Then shadowed him through the doorway.

"Come on in." He gestured.

"I'm already in."

He recoiled. "Where'd you come from?"

"The RSL bar silly." She giggled as she fought to keep her balance. "Don't ya remember?"

"Right." He shot out an unsteady finger at her.

She snatched it, shoved her body into his, and

collapsed them both to the floor in fits of ridiculous laughter.

Max sat up, not quite making it off the floor. "You ok love?"

Love? "Yeah." She snickered and snorted.

"That's good. Because I don't want to have sex with an injured woman."

She hurled her handbag at him. "That's lovely that is."

"Aw come on Jeannie."

"Jenna."

"Right."

Jenna stood up, and ran her palms down her skirt. They didn't have much work to do since the skirt was short. Very short. "A mini-skirt," she'd told Max at the bar when he'd enquired. A short, tight, black mini-skirt. Topped off with a short, tight, pink t-shirt. She'd hinted at a tour and possibly something more. And about three and half hours of drinking later, it grew into an unwritten promise.

Max was easy pickings. Low hanging fruit.

"Maxy." She pouted as she leaned down towards him and grated a poorly manicured fingernail down his shoulder – like a nail down a blackboard. "I know we haven't known each other long-"

Max cut her off, and stuck three fingers in her face. Then added one with his other hand. *Four hours.*

She rolled her eyes at him. "But I'd appreciate it if you would get my name right." She smiled wide and fake.

Max lowered his eyes in sheepish submission. "Sorry love."

Love? There it was again. But she ignored it.

Jenna turned and stalked to the other side of the room, one long black boot in front of the other.

Max, still on the floor, shoved the door shut, then watched his newly acquired date, with a cautious eye. She huffed as she turned and headed right for him – a panther, after its prey.

Cripes! His heart beat a little faster.

Then she stopped suddenly and hovered over him. "I forgive you Maxy." She giggled her sexy best, making her intentions for the night clear.

The chop and change confused Max. Much like it had earlier that night.

He had met Jenna at the local RSL earlier that evening. A pint sized, sexy little number that got him all hot under the collar, as he watched her dance up a storm on the small, square corkboard that doubled as a dance floor.

He'd caught her as she'd vibrated off the dance floor and offered her a drink.

"Drink?" he'd asked, indicating his own beer in his hand and clinked it against another full bottle – he'd ordered a spare just in case.

He'd had a miserable day at work and on this Friday night, he was set to forget. "Women!" He'd muttered to the barely interested fellow next to him at the bar. "Always gotta watch whatch…what you say. So sensitive." He'd raised an eyebrow as if bringing home the point. "They don't know when they got somethin' good."

Then he had spotted Jenna on the dancefloor – then a lightning 180 degrees later – "Hey baby!" And he didn't take his eyes off her until she'd left the dance floor.

"No," she'd said with a pre-programmed shake of her head. "I do not want a drink." She'd almost completely passed him by, when she'd abruptly turned around and added. "Ok." And she had smiled so sweetly at him with those big brown eyes and long, flapping lashes.

He was weak. That was true. But he wasn't desperate. *No sir, he was not desperate.* He knew he was a catch for the ladies. At almost six foot, he was no slouch himself. Wavy, sandy-brown hair – which at thirty-six was still mostly all there – and then there was his beefy bod, bad guy goatee and his lumberjack styled clothes. He was a real man – a solid man, inside and out. *That's what women really want.* And that's what he gave them – *a real man.*

Max pried himself up off his floor and squared off face-to-face with Jenna. *Was sobriety kicking in?* He took her hand in his and led her into the lounge room. She pulled loose from his grasp and flung herself onto the large, soft cushions that made up his lounge.

"Oh, how delightful." Her tone melodic.

He watched captivated, as her body melted into the cushions. *God she was sexy!*

Jenna's blonde hair fell loose around her shoulders and contrasted against the chocolate coloured fabric of the lounge.

She stretched out across the obliging cushions.

Max stood immobile. The sight of her was enticing – delectable. He wouldn't be able to resist for long.

He watched entranced, as her short skirt began to

ride up her slender thighs. Then he noticed...*I don't think she's wearing any knickers*...and it was just a little bit too delicious and he was just a little bit too hungry.

He felt himself harden, and strangely...he felt a desire to please this woman. He checked that. *Yes, he actually wanted that.* Maybe it was just his ego talking, but the desire to satisfy this woman was definitely present.

He shook his heavy boots from his feet, and plucked his flannelette shirt from his jeans, and tossed it, leaving only his black t-shirt underneath. The night was warm, but the alcohol had made him even more hot and sweaty.

A few hasty steps brought him closer to her. His heart raced.

Jenna flung her arms above her head and stretched out like a cat, pushing her chest up in the air.

Max saw the outline of her breasts begging to him through her flimsy t-shirt and then he saw...*nipples.*

He felt his control slip. *Really, he had control?* He advanced towards her, heart beating, penis throbbing. She was one sexy piece of crumpet, teasing him like that, and he was not going to wait any longer.

***

Katherine retrieved her book from the pillow. Now rugged up, warm and winter cosy, she snuggled into bed, pulled up the lusciously soft, white doona, flattened down her book at the last page she was on, located the line she was up to and started reading again.

'She no longer smelled the perfume from the

powder room flowers. The hot scent of the stranger in the tuxedo overwhelmed the soft, delicate aroma of the helpless blooms. She felt it pull her towards him like a magnet to its mate.

He reached out and gently lifted her hand. Then he traced the length of her arm until his fingers touched her bare shoulder. Her body tingled as the excitement swelled inside her. His fingers brushed along her neck, looping an escaped curl around them. He toyed with it for a second, just enough to suspend his touch, sending shivers down her spine. Then with an open palm, he rubbed his hand along the back of her neck, gently caressing her skin.

She felt the heat from his touch – her body responded.

God it felt good. She was under his spell.

He moved a hand to her face and ran the back of his fingers down her cheek, his touch like a feather. She closed her eyes. Then he leaned in towards her and brushed his lips against hers. A shot of excitement erupted through her body.

God! Weakness sapped her strength. She faulted and might have collapsed in a limp heap if he hadn't reached out to hold onto her. And when he did, she felt the strength in his hands, in his arms. For a second, she imagined what it would be like to be held hard against him. She shivered.

His eyes locked onto hers, as he gently pushed her back towards the bench, securing his body in front of her.

Cornered.

He leaned into her and trailed light kisses down her

neck and across her shoulder. She couldn't escape. Then he traced a finger along the top of her breasts.

God what was she doing? But she knew she couldn't stop now – didn't want to stop now. An inaudible thought tried to break into her consciousness – *what if someone walks in?* But the thought didn't take hold.

The string quartet below started playing again, signalling the end of one speech, and the start of another. She caught her breath. *Was that the last speech before hers?* She'd thrown time and caution to the wind.

His kisses rained down over her shoulder, and at some point she'd realised – and she was oblivious to when it had happened – he had turned her around.

Smooth. She found herself facing the benchtop and caught a glimpse of their reflections in the mirror above her. Excitement flashed through her veins like a dam bursting. She'd never experienced anything like it.

He leaned his full body against hers.

She felt the pressure of his firm body hard up against her – the mere sensation of it sent an explosion of electricity shocks splintering through her body. *Oh god!*

She felt his heat sear through the thin fabric of her dress. She was weak, excited and heavy with anticipation. She knew she was at his mercy – and she knew what was coming next.'

***

Max plonked down with too much force on the soft cushions of his lounge.

Jenna jumped, eyes open wide.

Max looked over his prize which was now stretched

out on his lounge. *His lounge. How did he get so lucky?*

Jenna watched him with seemingly little more than a mild interest. Still unsure which way the evening would go. *Or which way she'd let it go.*

Max bounced a little further along the lounge towards her.

She was pretty sure she knew which way he wanted it to go.

He leaned against her legs.

It reminded her of her cat pushing up against her when it wanted her attention. She smiled uneasy at the tomcat up against her now, doubtful he had what it took to do the job – not the least of which was that he was still mostly drunk – and stank of it too.

Max pushed himself harder against her legs. She had teased him all night, and now here she was – in his house – on his lounge, ready for the taking. He cast an eye over her body. He couldn't wait to fondle those boobs. *Couldn't wait to get started.*

She sighed to herself. *Might as well.* He might surprise her.

He saw a glimpse of a spark in her eye. The starter pistol had gone off. He shoved a clumsy hand under her t-shirt and slipped a hand inside her bra.

She caught her breath.

His other hand tried to release her bra clips. *Nearly have to be an engineer to undo these fucking things.*

She felt the rough edges of his skin scratch her breasts a little, and let out a squeak of delight…or it might have been shock.

God she felt good to touch. The silky smooth, warmth of her breasts incited an urgency inside him. His touching became more insistent till he was groping hard, across her nipples, trying to twist one.

She gasped at the sensation. She decided right at that moment – *yep, she probably had a quick draw McGraw on her hands.* Likely to lose control too early. She wanted to calm him down. She reached up and touched his shoulders, then ran her hands down his arms, trying to break his resolve a little.

"Maxy," she said with a heavy breath laced with uncertainty.

Her actions and the sound of her voice encouraged him. He wanted to please her. "Baby, I'm gonna give you the time of your life." He announced with intense genuineness.

Her eyes flew open again. Her heart beat faster – the anticipation…or again, shock.

In what seemed like one continuous movement, he pulled his hand out from under her shirt, unbuckled his belt, put both hands on her knees and pushed her legs apart.

***

'She stole a glance in the mirror again. *God it was too exciting for words. She should stop.* But she couldn't.

The man in the tuxedo – this hot, hot man that was making her melt – kept up his assault on her senses. He ran both hands down her waist.

She shivered again. The anticipation was unbearable. He secured his hands on the sides of her slim waist and followed the smooth fabric of her dress down to her thighs, sending currents of pleasure stinging through her body.

He expertly picked up handfuls of the soft, cool fabric, and lifted it slowly upwards until he could touch her bare skin underneath. He ran his hands along the edges of her lace panties. He didn't take them off – just pulled them aside – causing a sweet sensation across her clitoris.

Her body quivered in compliance. *God the pleasure.* Her eyes were hot and heavy. *She was ready for him – she was so ready.*

Her subconscious barely registered the sound of a bell in the distance, indicating the current speaker had only five minutes left to speak. She's next. *Yes she was next!*

She felt a sinful deliciousness being with this man – this stranger. The thrill of the forbidden made her pulse race as much as the anticipation of waiting for his next move. She placed her hands down firmly on the soft padding of the benchtop telling him she needed him.

He knew.

Then without warning, he whispered something in her ear. *French words.*

It shocked her – the only words he'd spoken. She didn't understand them – didn't care. His deep, husky tones made her body ache with savage, unrequited desire.

He groaned – an animal needing its release.

A shiver of fear and excitement shot through her.

He held onto the silken fabric of her skirt now above her waist and gently coaxed her legs to part. They obeyed willingly. He unzipped his tuxedo pants to release himself – he was full and hard. He slipped on a protective layer, and leaned into her.

She felt his hardness against her skin. *He's just there.* The excitement and thrill of what she was about to let happen burst from every fibre of her being. Her body responded. She caught her breath. She could wait no longer. She breathed out a deep, breathless moan.

It's all the sign he needed.'

***

Max ripped his fly down with the haste of a stray dog devouring a fresh bone. He couldn't wait any longer. He had to be inside her. The sight of her laying there, on his lounge, legs apart, in all her glory, was going to send him over the edge before he'd even started – and he didn't want to miss out on this. He hoisted himself up towards her, re-positioned his body, exposing his long, hard length.

Jenna gasped a throaty response, eyes wide at the sight of the looming hazard ahead.

Max was excited by her reaction and pleased that she liked what she saw. He fumbled as he slapped on a condom, and told her, "That's right baby. This is all for you."

He edged in closer towards her, penis taking aim towards its target.

Jenna's heart pumped hard – a cocktail of anticipation and uncertainty. She giggled nervously.

***

'The stranger gripped her arms, as she leaned down hard onto the benchtop. The sound of her breathless moan made him burn with rampant desire. He pulled her into him, then plunged deep into her.

She cried out. The brief shot of pain she felt quickly gave way to searing pleasure, and she gasped.

He thrust slowly, withdrawing to heighten her sensitivity and plunged back in. She whimpered and pressed her hands down harder on the benchtop. She lifted herself up onto her toes, and arched her back forward to allow him greater access. With each thrust he implanted inside her, she felt him.

It felt sexy. Naughty. Shameful even. But damn it felt good.

She felt him expand inside her – filling her. An urgent pressure rose up inside her. In the recesses of her mind, she was aware of the audience clapping downstairs, and the string quartet starting to play. *The current speaker had finished.*

She was momentarily shocked by the recollection of the audience downstairs. Shock turned to relief when she realised the noise of the conference was probably masking any sound coming from the powder room. Her eyes glazed over as she succumbed to the bliss overtaking her body.

He groaned with a guttural pleasure behind her. She responded with soft gasps each time his commanding thrusts hit their mark.

The pleasure was unspeakable. *Social etiquette be damned!*

***

Jenna looked up at Max hovering above her with searing intent in his eyes, and a throbbing penis in his hand. She saw it disappear out of view, then with no more warning, she felt him charge deep inside her. She cried out.

His left hand launched itself again under her shirt, this time, ripping it clumsily over her head, and tossing it to the floor. His hand hit home and again began its exploration of her breasts, as he thrust himself into her with hardening resolve.

She grabbed his hand and forced it down beside her. *Too rough.* She held onto his arms briefly, to calm him as he rocked hard against her.

The excitement was too much for Max to bear and he thrust strong pelvic grinds into her, over and over again.

She responded with deep groans and high pitched gasps as she tried to relax to take him in. *Fuck, he's a rabbit rooter!*

Her noises were music to his ears, and spurred him on even more. It excited him to satisfy a woman.

***

'The string quartet played louder to a crescendo, as she felt him suddenly pull half way out of her and then plunge back inside her for the last time deeper than before.

She let out a cry of delirious ecstasy and she could hold on no longer. She felt herself contract and release in quick succession over and over, slowly releasing the pressure from the unbearable burden.

He answered her by pushing in harder, only letting go when he released inside her, in the safety of the sheath.

His pulsing hardness heightened her own fulfilment

to an excruciating level. She felt her body go weak with the mini aftershocks of quivering pleasure that raced through her entire body.'

***

Max looked down at the sight of the sexy little hot number – Jenna, minus the pink t-shirt – that had teased him relentlessly all night long, and who was now wrapped around his penis.

"God you're sexy!" He exclaimed with a gruff satisfaction.

She smiled, barely able to speak, and gripped onto his lower back trying to anticipate every thrust and to take him in comfortably inside her. Her feet still in her boots, living up to their nickname – 'fuck me boots' – were planted firmly on the couch, in an effort to anchor herself for the ride.

She caught her breath and tried to find a rhythm with this man. Her head bumped against the arm of the lounge. She felt his hardness and his haste and she sunk her fingers into his torso even tighter to keep up with his seemingly endless desire.

"Oh god!" She cried out.

Max felt her holding on to him tighter. "You like that baby?" he said, happy to get confirmation that he was pleasing her, then proceeded to pound into her faster and harder. He knew how this worked. He needed to create the necessary friction in her soft areas.

She screamed out in surprise at the increased pace – maybe a little pleasure.

The sound of her cries told him what he needed to know. He's done his job. He has thrust deep and he has thrust hard and he can hold on no longer. "Baby, I'm gonna come!" He called out with one last plunge. "Come with me baby!"

Then as soon as he'd announced it, he groaned at the immense relief of pressure.

***

'The audience stopped clapping. The string quartet stopped playing. Her awareness shifted back to the conference downstairs. She froze. *Did they just call her name?* They were introducing her as the next speaker – the guest of honour.

The stranger withdrew from her body, causing ripples of sensation in his wake.

He put his arms around her gently holding her up. He then lowered her dress and smoothed it down for her. He turned her around, kissed her sweetly on the cheek, then again on the back of the hand. With a wry smile, he then escorted her to the door.

Her speech – he knows.

But she wasn't nervous anymore. And she needed no more preparation.

She retraced her path from the powder room, and descended the staircase at a casual pace belying the forbidden decadence in which she'd just indulged. She was just in time to hear her name being introduced again.

She slipped in between the tables at the back of the room, the point where she had escaped through in what seemed like only moments before. All eyes turned.

She strode up through the tables, towards the stage,

composed and confident – and she just knew that she was going to give a great speech.'

Katherine slipped a book mark in the book and snapped it shut. She sighed. *How exciting,* she thought with a dreamy smile on her lips as she drifted off to sleep.

***

Meanwhile, back at Max Martin's house:

Max breathed out heavy with relief. He had finished. He flopped down on top of Jenna. His penis remained inside her, while his puffing and panting wound down.

She smiled through gritted teeth as she held him close to her, trying to salvage her own pleasure while his climax subsided.

He lifted himself off of her and sat on the floor nearby. He gave her a proud smile, then patted her left breast. "Baby you were amazing."

She pushed her skirt back down and gave him a hesitant smile. She remained still on the couch, looking up at the ceiling, trying to hide the less than satisfied ache in her 'soft areas'.

Chapter Three

Monday morning, Max Martin stepped out of his small, brick home.

He'd purchased his own home a few years ago just as the market started to tip into a downward slide. Like many, he'd lost some equity in the house's value, but figured he wasn't selling anytime soon, so he hadn't lost anything in real dollar terms. He was confident the market would turn around and the equity would catch up…eventually.

He'd worked hard to pay his mortgage down and by his own calculations, in just under ten years' time, he'd own his house outright.

He scanned his front yard. *Bit of work to do.* He was happy to mow and whipper snip, but he hated gardening and weeding – *women's work.* This of course resulted in his lawns being neatly mowed and clipped, but his gardens, overgrown and terribly neglected. The old, brick edged gardens had come with the house. He did intend to hire someone to fix them up, but he'd yet to do a thing about them.

Max turned the key in his front door, locked it, then strolled along the cracked, concrete path that led to his driveway. He jiggled the set of keys in his hand, pressed a thumb into one of the key pads, and heard the deep clunk of locks releasing.

He eyed the late model, oceanic blue Colorado truck sitting in his drive – his pride and joy. With great ado, he slid into the driver's seat, twisted a key in the ignition and the engine roared to life. *Man's car.*

He eased back against the leather and savoured the lingering new car smell. He loved his truck – the only diversion from paying off his mortgage – apart from his fishing boat in his shed.

It was 7:00 a.m. on a disgustingly, hot and steamy day in the sunshine state of Queensland. He blasted the air-conditioner to ice and shoved the gearstick forward. Work beckoned.

As he turned out of the driveway and onto the street, his thoughts drifted back to Friday night and the great time he'd had with *Jenna*. He shook his head. He just couldn't believe his luck.

Was he whistling?

He felt an unexpected stirring in his groin just thinking about her. Sweet memories – how she looked sprawled across the couch. How her boobs looked and felt when he tore off her shirt. Being inside her. *Fuck she was hot.* He re-arranged himself. Sure, she wasn't the kind of girl he'd take home to meet the family, but he definitely saw himself hooking up with her again.

Big dog's gotta eat.

As he took the next left out of his street, he passed a large, open park on the left, smiled at the dog training session being conducted on the oval, and drove on through an intersection. He pulled up in front of a low-set modern Queenslander boasting immaculately maintained gardens on all sides of the house, as far as the eye could see.

Max grinned. "Pussy!"

The front door opened, and the house's occupant appeared – Gary Balderson.

Gary gently closed the door of his house behind him and light stepped along the neatly laid, stone path, before slipping through a little swing gate, letting it clink closed behind him.

He approached the truck. "Hey mate." He greeted Max with a full beam of a smile before sliding his slim body into the passenger seat.

Next to Max, Gary looked short, but he wasn't. He might not have been as tall or well-built as Max, but he definitely held his own.

Max smirked a greeting. "Baldo." Then he cast a suspicious eye over his passenger's outfit.

His mate flashed him a warning. "Don't even say it Max."

Max tried – he really did – but a shot of laughter imploded in his throat.

"I don't have to keep defending my choice of clothes to you?" Gary waved an arm over himself as if he was sweeping for a wire. "I gotta look good for my customers ok."

"Your customers don't care how you look mate. They just wanna see the bike gear you sell. You should wear that more often. Nobody wears fuckin' suits in this town." Then he chuckled again. "Maybe you should get a job at Seaworld as a fill in for a penguin."

Gary scowled at him. "Well, I'm the boss." He pointed to his multi-coloured shirt and matching tie. "I gotta set an example."

He shot a sneer at Max's typical get up of t-shirt, shorts and steel cap work boots. *It was usually thongs.* "Not like you."

"Uh-huh." Max pulled out from the curb, performed a perfect u-turn and drove back towards the intersection.

"Besides…I do wear the bike gear sometimes."

"When?"

"Casual Fridays – once a month." He explained, his tone defensive. "It's good for staff morale."

Max shot out a rough laugh. "You're the only fuckin' staff that has to change clothes for casual Fridays. Everyone else is already casual!"

"Well not all of us can dress like hobos at work." He flicked a hand and grinned. "Just drive will you."

The two friends carpooled – they both worked in town. And they both lived in Granville – a sort of offshoot from the main town of Maryborough – and referred to by naysayers as 'little Bronx', presumably because of an historical perception of its once lower socio-economic population.

Polar opposites, Max and Gary had been mates since primary school. Each man had their own circle of friends, and frequently they absolutely did not intersect. Gary had once left town for the big city of Brisbane, but when he came back, they simply picked up where they'd left off. Somehow their friendship worked – most days.

Gary shuffled in his seat. "So how was your weekend?" He glanced at Max.

Max replied with a knowing grin. Then he forced a wide smile, intended to conceal nothing.

"What? You're kidding?" His eyebrows sprang up. "Unbelievable. How do you do it?"

"What do ya mean how do I do it?"

No reply.

"You make it sound like I'm an ugly prick or something."

"No mate." He snickered.

"Come on…what then?"

He sniffed for effect. "It's just, seriously, I don't how you do it."

"Do what? What are you talking about Baldo?"

"Nothin' hey." He shook his head. "Just drop it." He preferred not to say. Max could be really horrible to women sometimes – and yet he still managed to convince them to sleep with him.

Max glanced at his passenger, then snapped his eyes back to the road. *Ok.*

They drove without speaking, passing over the Granville bridge heading into town. The river level was low – the Mary River. The water was filthy brown and muddy, yet somehow its wide span and slow current made it seem serene and inviting. Of course, less inviting were the persistent stories of crocodiles in the river, supported by the rare news coverage that one had been captured and relocated.

The bridge was one of two in town that flooded, seemingly lately on a regular basis. It was an interesting quagmire that the Mary River ran downstream from

Gympie, which was the next big town an hour south. If it rained hard enough in Gympie, it flooded in Granville. When the bridge flooded, residents were cut off – stranded.

"Did you watch the footy Saturday night?" Max asked, breaking the ice again.

"Yeah the Broncos played good – twenty-four to nil."

Max nodded, impressed.

"Hear Fletcher's fighting down the bay next month. We should go see it."

Max's eyes lit up. "Yeah that'd be good." He loved boxing.

Gary didn't, but he'd go with him. The only fights Gary got into growing up were the ones that Max dragged him into – usually drunken teenage brawls. *Gotta stand by your mates.*

Max pulled up in front of "Baldo's Bikes", Gary's own store. His mate had set up his business seven years ago, selling motorbikes, accessories and parts. Business was steady. Motocross and dirt bike riding were big sports in the area and popular with the town's youth.

A sudden thought struck Max. "Maybe I can find a date for you…for the fight?"

Gary opened the door. "Fuck off mate." He grinned as he slid out of the truck. "I wouldn't trust you to pick a woman for me." He tapped the top of the roof a couple times, shut the door and waved. "See you later mate. Don't leave me waiting again this afternoon."

Max smiled. "No worries." He returned the wave,

laughing at himself as he spun around the corner to his own workplace.

A minute later, he stopped in front of "The Outboard Shop". Then turned left into a wide gravel driveway, and parked in one of the spaces reserved for employees. He grabbed his gear and jumped out of the truck.

He pushed the keypad on his set of keys again and heard the deep clunk of the locks going back into position. He hit it again, the brief horn blast signalling that the truck was indeed locked – good and proper. Max mused at the noise.

The Outboard Shop consisted of a large retail store which sold all manner of boating accessories, and a huge work shed out the back where mechanical works were carried out on boats and outboards that customers brought in.

Max strolled towards the shed – his workplace. He could hear the boys at work already and the smell of outboard fumes wafted out. *Someone's just run a motor.*

Max was one of two fully qualified outboard mechanics that worked here, along with a second year apprentice. The yellow and blue sign over the shed listed a motley crew of work they performed:

'Motor Services and Repairs
Prop & Prop Repairs
Engine Installs, Maintenance & Repairs
Pre-purchase Inspections
Customised Fit-outs'

Custom fit-outs were Max's claim to fame. He had started out on the basics like all eager young mechanics, but Max had stood out from the pack early. He was hungrier, hardwired to achieve and his work ethic was relentless.

He bulldozed his way through the first few years of work and now fifteen years later, he all but managed the shed. "I can't spell big words, but I can lift heavy things." He liked to joke.

But that wasn't entirely true. His ability to invent practical solutions for customers had earned him the trust and respect of his colleagues and boss. No, Max's work ethic and capabilities were definitely not the problem.

He nodded to his co-workers – Rob and Kyle – as he approached the oversized shed. Then noticed the apprentice struggling with a propeller – almost dropping it.

"Careful with that fucking prop will ya Kyle?" He shot the youth an icy glare.

Kyle's mop of curly hair hung almost in his eyes.

"You drop that and you'll bend the blades, and it'll be a fuck around to fix it."

The apprentice flicked the mop out of his eyes. "Yeah no worries mate." But the embarrassment had momentarily stung him.

Max shook his head, then sidled up to the tinnie he planned to get to work on. He'd started the job last week – still had to fix the tinnie's hydraulic steering system. He grabbed a spanner and started digging around in the centre console. *Wrong spanner.*

"Kyle!"

The apprentice flung his head around and scooted over.

Max held out the spanner. "Put this back and grab me the ten mil open ender." He demanded. "I need it quick, so chop chop."

Kyle brought back the spanner and handed it up to Max.

He grabbed it. "Thanks mate."

The new recruit grinned, this time taking the senior mechanic's abrupt orders on the chin, and returned to his previous task.

Max was absorbed in his work, breaking his concentration only to emit the odd grunt, huff or curse. *Need to get this job finished by lunch.* He removed the hydraulic line which leaked out hydraulic fluid all over his hands.

"Fuck." He searched for a rag and growled at the delay.

"Excuse me," a shaky, female voice called out.

It came from the entrance to the shed. Nobody in the shed responded.

"Ah, excuse me." The woman called out again with more urgent fervour.

She took her floppy sun hat off and fanned herself with it. The stifling, muggy heat threatened to stick her entire sundress to her small frame.

Max glanced up, the surprise echoed in his voice. "What do you want?"

She took a step back. "Sorry."

He squinted out into the sun's glare to see her.

She shoved her hat back on. "Um…the guy in the shop there said to come out back and see…ah…Max."

'The guy in the shop' was Frank – Max's boss. He owned and managed The Outboard Shop.

Max huffed. "What's it about? I'm busy right now." He turned back to the hydraulic line in his hand and tugged to release it from the console.

The woman watched as the man in the boat turned his back to her. *Men.*

She scanned the shed for any other shred of help. *Nothing.* She hated these environments – *bunch of men* – always made her feel uncomfortable.

Her eyes drew back to her one apparent hope.

Max felt her hot stare on him – but he barely turned to look at her. "Can you come back after lunch?"

"No, not really." She shook her head and took an uneasy step forward. "The guy in the shop said you'd be able to help me. Said it wouldn't take long. Just a quick question really." She paused trying to keep her manner polite. "I just need to know what size stainless steel prop I can buy for my husband's outboard."

She glanced up at the man in the tinnie, and shielded her face from the sun. Then as if she felt like she had to explain herself further. "It's a surprise – birthday present."

Max unwrapped the new hydraulic line which was intended to replace the old one he'd just pulled out. He still had to fit it, then bleed the hydraulic steering.

The woman flung her hands down by her side. *God he was ignoring her.* She felt a surge of stress rise up inside her. "He said it wouldn't take long." Her voice more urgent. "He said you'd be able to advise me pretty quickly."

Max glanced at the woman again, then back to the new hydraulic line that he'd just unwrapped. He realised they'd sent him the wrong one. "For fuck's sake!"

The woman took a step back. Shocked.

Max looked over at her as if he'd just noticed her for the first time. *Attractive.* But she was clearly not going away.

He ran an oily hand down his t-shirt, wetting any remaining dry spots with the transparent liquid. Then he slapped the dirty rag down onto the floor of the boat. "Alright love. I'll be there in a minute."

Frank was right. It only took him a few minutes to tell the woman what she needed to know. Then it was back to work as usual.

***

At the end of the work day, Frank summoned Max into his office.

"Listen Max." He ran a thick hand through his thinning hair.

"This can't be good." Max shoved his hands in his shorts' pockets. He breathed the cool office air as he glanced around the room. The office was drab and old but it had all the basics.

Frank gestured in the direction of the spare chairs. "Sit down."

He did.

"I've had a complaint." Frank eased himself down into a chair behind his desk.

Max grunted. "What kind of complaint?"

"Mrs Cameron."

"Who?"

His boss pointed in the general direction of the shed. "The lady who wanted to know about the props."

He nodded. "Yeah yeah. The woman from this morning. I told her which prop she needed. What? She wasn't happy with the advice?"

Frank shook his head. "No. She was perfectly happy with the advice." He shot a look at the wall for inspiration.

"For fuck's sake Frank, just spit it out will ya."

"Mate." His boss swiped a hand over his cheap tie. "You're my best mechanic."

"And that's a problem?"

"Of course not." He rubbed his forehead. *Really hate this part of the job.*

Max leaned forward in his chair. "Well what is it then?"

"Mrs Cameron said you were…." *Tread carefully.* "Off hand with her today. Said it made her uncomfortable."

Max sprang to his feet. "I knew it! Unbelievable. I've got a fucking job to do Frank!" He shook his head, eyebrows furrowed. "You send some sheila out to me in the middle of that, I can't help it if she has to wait."

Frank pressed his palms flat on the desk. "It's not the first time Max. You've got a reputation for treating women…." *He had to say it.* "Disrespectfully."

Max glared at him. "What the fuck Frank? I love women."

"Lower your voice. I still have customers out there."

"I'm not going to fuckin' lower my voice Frank."

"Will you stop swearing at me!" His tone was

harsh.

Max's eyes grew wide. *Frank rarely raised his voice.* He breathed deep and sat back down. "Sorry mate."

His boss lowered his voice too. "Look, I don't like this any more than you. But the gist of the complaints is that you're a bit of a chauvinist…with women." He was quick to add. "Of course I know that's not true-"

Max cut him off. "Complaints? There's more than one?" It was like a sledgehammer.

"Max-"

But he was on the defensive again. "What do you mean a chauvinist? Like a male chauvinist?"

Frank's expression was pained. "There's another kind?"

"Aw come on Frankie." He huffed. "You know me. That's not who I am."

"I know that Max." *Most of the time.* "But…you actually can be a bit harsh with women." *And men too for that matter.*

He leaned forward, his voice reassuring. "I'm on your side Max. I truly am. But I can't afford to lose customers or for my business to get a reputation for being unfriendly to women. They may not be a big part of our customer base, but you still have to treat them with respect."

Max toyed with a pencil on the desk, leaving oily fingerprints on its edges. "What do you want me to do about it Frank?"

"Just…try to make a better effort with our female customers."

"I didn't think I was that bad."

Frank flicked him a strained look.

"Okay okay." Max raised his hands in surrender. "I'll try and be better."

"Thank you. I appreciate that."

"Is that it?"

He nodded. "Yeah. That's it."

Max leapt out of his chair. "Ok then. See you tomorrow Frankie."

"Yeah." He watched him march out the door.

Max stormed over to his truck, the conversation he'd just had with his boss still scathing in his mind. *Women. It's always the women.*

He sped out of the gravel carpark and headed towards Baldo's Bikes. He found his mate closed up and waiting outside the front door.

Gary walked over to the truck and jumped into the passenger seat. He saw his mate's downtrodden expression. "What's up?"

"Fuck all. Let's grab a beer?"

"Sure."

As they drove around the next turn, they passed a gaggle of young women sitting, alfresco style, at the "Café on Kent".

The women were clearly absorbed, giggling over some well-guarded secret. The lead woman appeared to be showing the others something in a paperback book.

Max stopped at a red light, hit the button to slide down Gary's window, then he narrowed his eyes and shook his head. "Women."

"Chicks hey?" Gary offered.

"Yeah." Max eyed the group. "Women. I mean what the fuck are they laughing at?"

Gary shrugged, then released a boyish grin. "Probably reading that porn shit they're all sneakin' around with these days."

"What?" His eyes wide with shock. "What do ya mean?"

Gary's expression turned sheepish. He willed Max to understand without having to explain it to him.

But his mate drew a blank.

Gary rolled his eyes. "Oh for the love of-. You know. That 'mummy porn' stuff."

"What are ya talkin' about Baldo?"

"Sex! Kinky shit. For women!" He yelled, then immediately shrank down in his seat when a passerby frowned at him.

He blew out a breath. Then lowered his voice as if he was telling Max a dirty secret. "They love it."

The light turned green and Max took off again. He frowned. "How do you know that?"

He flushed with embarrassment. *Crap.* "Yeah alright. That girl I dated last year – Tanya. She bought those books." He fidgeted in his seat. "She ah…wanted us to 'read it together'." He used air quotes to emphasise the point.

Max laughed. "Was that before or after you bought your Taylor Swift CD?"

"Shut up. Of course I didn't read them – the books I mean." *Or buy the CD.*

They let an uncomfortable moment pass.

"Seriously." Gary went at it again as if he felt the need to maintain a defence. "It's all the rage. Women love it hey."

Max had no markers in the sand. He shook his

head.

"Mate it's true. Didn't any of those women you brought home ever mention it?"

Max snorted. "Fuck no." Then he thought about it. "We never did much talkin' mate."

Chapter Four

Katherine had dreams – big dreams. Her mother once told her that her head was too far up in the clouds. *'Don't aim so high honey. I don't want you to be disappointed.'*

But that was a long time ago. No-one said that to Katherine now.

"Kat!" her housemate's voice echoed up the stairs, breaking her reverie.

"Nearly ready!" She shuffled some papers in order and layered them into a file that was spread out on her bed. She'd fallen asleep working again – *distracted by that book*. A tingle of excitement flittered through her when she thought about finishing it tonight.

"Come on girl. We're gonna miss that bus."

She knew Sally would be pacing at the front door.

They didn't always catch the bus together – usually only on Mondays. Katherine had an early staff breakfast meeting every Monday morning to discuss the week's work, which meant travelling into the city on the same bus as her housemate. *Today was Monday.*

She'd never been one of those people that hated Mondays. She heard a lot of people say they did though – *'Mondyitis – 'it's Monday', groan."* Usually accompanied by whiney, miserable faces – but not Katherine. She loved work. Always did. Same as school – she loved that too.

In a final flurry of activity, Katherine zipped up her skirt, shoved her feet into her day heels and grabbed a matching grey jacket. She snatched up her handbag, keys and sunglasses, double checked that her 'special' book was still secured under the messy pile of socks in the second drawer of her dresser, made a mental note to buy that reading tablet – then hurried out the bedroom door.

The two housemates flew out the front door and spilled onto the footpath. The heat in the air already starting to warm them too much.

"I really don't like Summer." Sal looked skywards.

They marched like power walkers through the little suburb's streets. Too many times they cut it too fine. It took ten minutes to get to the bus stop – then another fifty to the city. Some days they cursed living so far south of Brisbane. But to get an affordable place in a nice area meant living out of the city, and commuting in.

Their satellite estate was friendly, fresh and lush. It was only twenty-one kilometres from the city, but as traffic on the roads was chronically congested, the trip in by car could be as long as two hours on a bad day. Best option was to bus it.

If luck was on their side, there wouldn't be any delays on the freeway today. Once the bus made it into the designated busway, it was practically express all the way to the city.

Trickles of residents from the tiny suburb funnelled towards the only bus stop near the entrance of the estate, where a massive stone structure identified the estate as "Waterstone".

Katherine's heels clicked along the bitumen road, till they made their way back up to where the cement footpath began.

Sally frowned at her. "You really should think about wearing sneakers till you get to work. A lot of people do it." She sounded like an advertisement and pointed to her own bright white shoes, just as she side-stepped a small pile of dog business.

Katherine grinned at the near miss – and at how mismatched the flashes of white looked against Sally's brown and yellow uniform. "Yes, well they do look comfortable."

Sally managed a coffee shop. The uniform was a necessity and Katherine knew her friend hated the colours – they were too drab. *Like a big ol' coffee bean.*

The thought made her smile.

"What are you smiling at?"

"Nothing."

Sally's coffee shop was on the ground floor of the building where Katherine worked. It's how they met.

"You know Kat, when I think about it, in the two years I've known you, I've yet to see you wear anything other than heels…or slippers." She giggled.

An oncoming passerby hogged the footpath, making no attempt to move over. Katherine quickly leaped off the footpath, over the dewy grass, and landed on the edge of the gutter – like two cars on a skinny road, someone had to put two wheels on the dirt.

Sally scrambled over to join her. "Some people need to learn how to share." She huffed, then added. "See that would have been easier if you were wearing sneakers."

Her friend pulled her lips tight then shook her head. "I just don't like wearing flats Sal – makes me feel short and under dressed."

"But you're not that short. You're taller than me."

That wasn't hard when Sally stood five foot nothing.

Sally rolled her eyes. "Ok." *Change the subject.* "What about Steven? Is he tall?"

Katherine looked away, sucked her lips in as if locking in the information. "I'm not discussing Steven with you." She glanced up to see if the bus was in the distance, but couldn't hide the smile emerging across her lips.

Sally saw it. "Why not?"

"Because it will jinx it alright?" She blushed.

"Are you blushing?"

A trio of male joggers in tank tops and flappy shorts swept past them. The sight made them twitter like school girls after the trio passed by.

Sally snickered. "Seriously, what's with the flapping shorts?"

Her friend jutted an elbow into her ribs. "Behave."

Sally lowered her voice as if she had uncovered a great secret. "So you do like him? Steven I mean."

No response. Just a swish of a long, brown ponytail.

"You can't fool me Katherine Wilkins. You always

swish your ponytail when you're keeping secrets."

Katherine chuckled. "What? I do not." She swished her ponytail again. "I'm not discussing this with you."

"Well then." Sally's hand instinctively patted the tight, blonde bun on the back of her head. "Fine. Don't talk about it. I won't talk about…Bruce."

Katherine burst into laughter. *There's no Bruce.* "Ok." She relented, the pout on Sally's face sealing the deal. "Fine. He's nice ok. Steven's nice."

"Nice!"

"Shh!" Katherine stumbled, catching herself before she buckled completely. She frowned. "What's wrong with nice?"

"Good god Kat, it's the kiss of death." She spied the old bus coming down the street up ahead. *The freakin' rattler.*

"What are you talking about?"

"Seriously Kat, no guy worth having is 'nice'." She was distracted, calculating if they would make it in time. A line of people started to form at the bus stop, so she figured they'd hail the bus first. *Buys another couple minutes.*

Katherine shook her head. "You're nuts you know that. I don't believe that."

Her housemate raised her hands in surrender. "Ok, your life." Then with a touch more urgency. "Bus is coming."

Katherine ignored her, distracted. "See this is why I don't talk to you about this stuff. There's nothing wrong with 'nice'."

Her friend shoved her with a playful grin on her

face. "Come on! We'll miss the bus."

***

Later that morning, Katherine settled into a single booth at "The Bean n' Stalk" coffee shop, in the lobby of the building where she worked.

Her staff meeting had wrapped early and the office was fast becoming a hive of activity – a very noisy hive. There was a gap in her diary, so she'd seized the chance for some quiet time.

She'd scooped up a couple current files off her desk, and made a beeline for the elevator, then stepped inside the safety of its mirrored walls.

Once the elevator hit the bottom, she'd walked out into the huge, expansive lobby. The building impressed her – it was big – forty floors. She saw others with the same idea working in nearby booths.

It was easy to see why people set up makeshift work booths at The Bean n' Stalk. Not only was it a reprieve from the distractions in the office, it was an excellent networking opportunity. Both private and government offices operated in the building – including accountants – *Steven* – and they all needed coffee.

The Bean n' Stalk was typically swamped by a flood of office workers around 10:00 a.m. – morning tea time – and again mid-afternoon.

Katherine flashed Sally a short wave. Her friend bustled about behind the frosted glass servery area, which boasted the shop's distinctive range of fresh salads – *the Stalk*.

Sally caught the acknowledgement. She knew her housemate's order by heart. *Always the muffin of the day.*

Katherine gazed out over the massive foyer taking in the glittering, glass and granite décor. She smiled with delight. *Who wouldn't love this building?* The extraordinarily high ceilings created the sense that sound was being sucked upwards – making an ideal work acoustic below.

Informal business meetings sprang up like mushrooms along the adjacent wall. Black lounge chairs and wooden tables were strategically placed along the floor-to-ceiling glass walls, treating visitors to spectacular river views. *Who wouldn't want to work here?*

She allowed herself one last visual indulgence – the stunning art exhibition that lined the path to the coffee shop.

She closed her eyes and drew in a satisfied breath – she heard the last of the morning's soft melodies float out of the grand piano. *Only in a building like this.* The piano was an exquisite luxury that adorned the entrance of the building, prominently placed between two thick, polished steel columns.

Yes, the effect of being on the ground floor was a definite eclectic treat for the senses. The building felt alive – and Katherine loved it!

"You're latté and blueberry muffin, Madam." Sally giggled as she placed the mug and plated muffin on the table.

Katherine smiled as she heard her friend's feet clink about on the granite floor. "Nice shoes."

She grinned as she placed a serviette and cutlery beside the muffin plate.

"Thanks Sal." She moved the plate to the side. "I'd ask you to sit, but I know you're not scheduled to take a break until later."

"That's ok. I know you've got work to do anyway," she said with a coy grin as she slipped into the booth, seating herself firmly beside Katherine.

Her friend's eyes flashed wide with surprise.

"It's ok. Stace will cover for me." She flung a short wave to the other girl behind the counter then made herself comfortable. "Put your pencil down, I wanna talk to you for a sec."

"Couldn't this wait till later?"

"Just quickly." Sally assured her.

She placed her pencil ceremoniously on the copy she was marking up. "If the next word out of your mouth is-"

"About Steven," they said at the same time.

Sally cut in quickly. "Well, since you brought it up."

I didn't.

She pulled her order pad out of her pocket.

"You're taking notes?"

"No." She giggled. "I just want to look like I'm…you know, getting feedback from you…a customer."

"You're the manager."

"So? What's your point?"

Katherine shook her head. She didn't always have time to figure Sally out. "Whatever. Look, what is it? I'm busy."

Her friend toyed with the order pad. "See that's the thing Kat. You're always busy." She pulled at the corners of the pad. "You're always working, studying or something. You're so quiet all the time…and secretive – I don't know what you're doing up there in your bedroom for hours." She made a zip across her lips with her fingers and pretended to toss away a key. "Hey, none of my business."

Katherine rolled her eyes. *Jesus.*

"It's just…Kat…that you don't seem to be having much fun. You hardly ever go out with a man."

She raised a hand to protest. "That's not true. I went out with Steven the other night."

She lowered her eyebrows. "Kat, Steven doesn't count."

Her friend leaned back. "How can you say that? You don't know anything about him."

"I know he's boring…too boring for you."

"What?" Katherine hissed, trying to keep the sound down. "Just because I said he was nice?"

Sally nodded. "Yes, that. And because I know the type that you go after. Safe and boring."

Katherine's mouth twisted into a scowl. "What's wrong with safe and boring?" She shook her head to correct herself. "Steven's not boring."

Sally patted her housemate's hand. *She clearly needed her help.* "Honey. I believe you need more excitement in your life. Now look. There's this guy-"

Katherine cut her off. "I see where this is going." She dragged her hand out from under Sally's. "You want to set me up with some weirdo." She whispered too loudly.

"No." Sally's eyes ventured left then right. "No. I do not. He's not a weirdo. I was just talking with my friend Justine about him and-"

"I knew it." Katherine picked up her pencil and held up a hand for Sally to stop. "I've got work to do."

"Ok." Sal paused for dramatic effect. "Just think about it."

Katherine whacked her on the arm with her own order pad. "Go."

"Ok, I'm going." She got up to leave. "But remember – perfect's not out there Kat. It's just real messy. That's when you know it's real."

She'd heard her friend say this many times before. She watched as Sal started to walk away. Then as if they were in high school, her friend spun back around, cupped her hand to her mouth and mouthed the words, "We haven't finished this discussion. Later."

We were having a discussion?

Katherine watched as the love guru sauntered back to her post.

She turned her attention back to her work, but her focus was gone. Somewhere in the recesses of her mind, her friend's words were etching their way in.

Was she really looking for something in a man that wasn't there? She liked a capable, intelligent man – sensitive and polite – and who paid particular attention to his grooming habits. *Steven was all that – wasn't he?*

Yes he was all that, of course he was.

But it didn't stop the slow and unwanted realisation that pushed its way into her consciousness.

Oh crap! Steven was boring.

Chapter Five

"Simon! Catch!" Max called out as he tossed the football to the junior player in the blue jersey, emblazoned with the number seven.

The little player caught the ball with a thud, the force winding him. He stood transfixed, bewilderment erupting across his face.

"Now pass it to Jack!" Max pointed to Jack who had been running alongside Simon.

Next he called out to Jack. "Jack, get ready to catch the ball!"

Jack, shocked by the sudden instruction to act, stopped running. His little possum face lit up with hope and expectation.

Max saw him stop. "Keep running Jack!" He waved an arm towards the wide expanse of the green field in front of them. "Catch the ball when Simon passes it to you."

Wanting to please his coach, even if it was only footy practice, Simon made a solid pass to Jack.

Max smiled. *Good pass Simon.*

Jack held the ball for a microsecond, then it slipped from his grasp. He made a gallant attempt, but ultimately failed to hold onto the rubber prize. He fumbled and dropped the ball in front of him, and it was a knock on, which gave the other team a penalty.

He saw his mistake. His little face twisted. His parents were watching. *Dad's going to be disappointed.* "I'm useless!" The little lad shoved a weak arm with a weaker fist on the end of it, into the ground, achieving nothing but dirty knuckles and a sore elbow.

Max jogged over to him. "Hey buddy. Don't beat yourself up. Happens to all of us." He flicked him a reassuring wink, and patted him on the back.

"Yeah," the little boy said without conviction, then he moved back into centre position. "Whatever you say coach."

Max hovered on the sidelines, watching his new young charges. Some of the kids' families were here today, and he knew that put a lot of pressure on them – sometimes unduly.

It had been a long, hot training session. Only now, the cool of the very late afternoon provided some relief.

The hardcore barrackers stood on the edge of the field – usually the fathers. Other spectators sat in various stages of disinterest, in the stands. The rows of old, weather beaten seats spread out along the length of the field looked like they'd been there forever.

Simon's dad, a burly man with a scruffy beard, waved to his son on the field. "Good pass son!"

Jack's father, a slender, wiry type, wasn't far away and agreed. "Yeah, your boy did good."

"Thanks mate." Then he nodded towards Jack on the field. "Don't worry about that fumble hey. Jack's improving."

Jack's father gritted his teeth when he thought about his son's poor performance. *Second place is for the first loser.*

"Listen, don't worry mate." Simon's dad told him. "That's why they called in ol' matey – Max Martin – to coach this season." He nodded towards Max. "He'll sort 'em out."

"He's new at coaching isn't he?" Jack's father looked out at Max in the field.

"Yeah mate. Coach Rowley's out for the season. Family stuff I think."

"This Martin fellow knows what he's doing ya think?" *Someone needed to sort out his son.*

"He should do."

"Why's that? You know him?"

"Yeah mate. Went to school with him. Fuckin' nothin' he doesn't know about football hey. Simon's happy."

"That's good then I suppose." He pointed to his son. "If he can straighten that one out, I'll be happy."

Jack noticed his father pointing at him. He felt beads of sweat start to form on his face.

Simon's dad glanced at Jack and then back to the boy's father. He pursed his lips but kept them shut. *One of those fathers.* Then he felt compelled to say, "It's about the game though isn't it? At their age. And having fun?"

Jack's dad barely nodded. *Sure it is.*

Conversation was over.

A sharp whistle sounded – Max called a break.

The players stampeded towards the table that held all the water bottles and arranged themselves in clumps, grabbing at the bottles.

Max held up a hand. "There's plenty for everyone."

The coach kept an eye on his players as he scooped up his own replenishment from his belongings now scattered along the ground near the sidelines. He moved them up a bit further towards the stands. A couple of parents accosted him with questions and plans for their kids in the team that year.

Simon's mother sat with her sister and a friend far back on one of the faded grey stands. It was way too hot to be spectators in the stands today. They fanned themselves with their broad straw hats and took frequent sips from their pink plastic bottles.

Two of the women looked noticeably out of place – dolled up in what better passed as nightclub gear. They were obviously overdressed for kids' football.

One of the women nudged her companion and giggled. She leaned in, lowered her voice till it was barely a whisper. "What about that one then? The coach? He's a bit alright."

Her companion sneered. "I don't think so."

"Are you crazy? What's not to want? Look at those legs…and that butt. Still looks pretty good for a guy his age." She winked. "He might be a bit of a goer in the sack."

Her cohort sniffed loudly, crossed her legs, slipped her hat back on her head, then glared down at the sidelines where the coach stood. Sure he looked ok – pretty good actually. In his sexy little footy shorts,

broad shoulders. A girl could get lost in those arms.
Yeah he definitely looked like he had the full package.

But her appreciation was short lived. She wasn't
going to tell her friend that she'd tried to get the
coach's attention earlier, only to have him pass her by
without a second glance. *Not even a hint of
acknowledgement as she walked by him.* She screwed up her
nose and pouted. "Don't bother." Her tone was harsh
and dismissive. "Doesn't look like he'd be that good."

Just then, a tiny hand wrapped itself around the
woman's ankle. The woman looked down and saw that
it belonged to Simon's little sister Annie.

The little hand tried to pull her into action. "Come
on Aunty Jenna. I wanna get an ice-cream."

***

The following day, Max Martin was back at work in
the shed of The Outboard Shop, ripping through the
line up of jobs on the docket for the day. The shed
burst with activity.

Max was intently focused on his current task –
removing a 150 horsepower outboard motor from a
seven metre, fibreglass boat. He was making short
work of it. The job had come in quickly because the
owner needed the motor replaced before the weekend.
Recreational fishers.

"Hey Rob." Max's face lit up as he called out to the
other mechanic.

"What?" Rob glanced up, he recognised the tone.
Max was in a good mood. *Here come the jokes.*

"Did you hear about the blonde business woman
who was driving in the outback and saw another

blonde sheila rowing a boat in a grassed paddock?"

Rob switched on a cheesy smile. "No mate."

"She pulled up and yelled out, 'It's dumb blondes like you that give us smart blondes a bad name.'" He grinned. "'If I could swim, I'd come over there and slap ya.'" He burst out a shot of laughter.

Rob chuckled.

The apprentice snickered – *when in Rome.*

They didn't care if Max's jokes were lame. He was in a good mood and that's all that mattered – they found the day ran smoother and less stressful.

The massive work shed was chock-a-block full of boats. Outboards on stands waited their turn. Two more boats sat on their trailers outside the shed, bearing the brunt of the hot summer heat, waiting to be brought in. And as soon as Max finished replacing the outboard on his current job, they could be.

Max had climbed up high into the tinnie to remove the old fuel filter from under the gunnel so he could fit a new one. He glanced around, lifting rags from the boat floor, shuffling gear. "Where's that new fuel filter?"

Kyle scouted around. "Dunno." He sprang over to a nearby workbench that was riddled with tools and equipment. "Not here. But I thought I saw it before."

"Just grab me another one will you."

Kyle scurried over to the store's cupboard at the back of the shed. "None left in here."

Max climbed out of the boat. "No worries mate." He stepped down onto the mudguard of the trailer and dropped to the oil-stained, cement floor. "I'll check if there's a spare in the shop."

As he left the cover of the shed, the instant hit of the frying, midday sun burned his arms. He quickened his step, crunching along the gravel path towards the back of the shop. He felt the sweat already pooling on his skin, and his shirt started to stick. *Fuck it's hot.*

He yanked open the back door and slipped through into the spare parts room.

At that same moment, a customer – a female customer – clad in tiny denim shorts with fraying edges, button up sleeveless shirt which exposed an ample cleavage – approached the front door, opened it and stepped inside. The electric buzzer sounded an alarm announcing the presence of a customer.

Tim Johnson the salesman, decked out in the shop's distinctive navy blue and yellow colours, duly responded.

"Can I help you Ma'am?" He said as he approached the lady. She perused the lifejackets on the rack against the wall and was yet to turn around. He moved closer towards her. Then he spotted, *butt cheeks* – poking out under the fraying edges of her shorts. He tried not to look down. *Jesus.* Unsuccessfully.

She turned around. Flashed him a sugary smile. "I sure hope so."

The salesman's jaw dropped as he saw…the next challenge – *cleavage.* "Of course I can…we can…we-"

She cut him off. "I'm looking for a lifejacket to fit my two year old niece."

"Ah sure." He fussed in the rack that held the little lifejackets. "Just can't see the one I'm looking for…." He breathed out – relieved to have a task to focus on. He bobbed around, looking left, looking right, his blonde hair flopping about as he searched. "I thought it was here yesterday." His nervous laughter made a fool of him. *Get a grip.*

She looked at him. "It's okay." Butter just melted. She pointed to the obligatory shop logo embroidered on his left pocket, just above his name "Tim Johnson". Then she smiled. "Cute."

The salesman stumbled. "My friends just call me 'Johnno'."

She whispered at him. "Of course they do."

He nearly fell into the rack of lifejackets, then was instantly startled by a shuffling noise in the back of the shop. He saw a shadow pass over the hall – a familiar shadow. "Max!" He called out, louder than necessary.

No answer.

Max had located a spare fuel filter on the top shelf and slid it off, catching it with a soft thud.

Tim smiled at his customer. "Excuse me a minute." He stepped into the back room, and whispered in a hurried tone. "Max."

Max snapped a glance in the direction of the voice. "What?"

"Did you guys pick up any of the kids' life jackets?"

Life jackets? Max took a step towards Tim, then another, until the salesman came into full view. "No mate." His voice was loud. "I overheard Frankie order some yesterday. Should be a couple left on the rack. Was yesterday."

Tim looked puzzled.

"Mrs Dawson asked me about them yesterday. Remember?" Max squinted at the salesman. "Don't you remember?" He circled the air with his index finger. "When she and her husband picked up their boat."

He watched Tim now with increased interest – *why is he squirming like a worm on a hook?* Suspicion mounting. "Why're you whispering Johnno?" *What's he hiding?*

He took a couple steps backwards so that the retail section of the store came into view. Then he saw it. *Short shorts.* And…*butt cheeks!*

Max's eyes narrowed further. "Timothy?"

Tim raised both palms. "Stop!" His voice a rushed whisper. "Keep away Max. You heard what Frankie said the other day." His voice grew firmer. "You don't need the trouble."

Max halted his advance. *The prick was right. He didn't need the hassle.* "No trouble mate." Then before he could make himself scarce, Butt Cheeks turned around and stared right at him. *Oops…can't leave now.*

"G'day love." He hoped he sounded professional. "Is Johnny boy here serving you alright?" *Fuck was he flirting with a customer?*

She folded her arms across her chest. "He is thank you." Her voice sterner than necessary. "And he's doing a very good job of it."

"That's good." Max nodded, then winked at her. "You just let me know then if he doesn't and I'll fix you right up." *What was he doing?* It wasn't Max's job to serve customers in the shop. He'd been warned by Frank that he had neither the manners nor cleanliness for it. Frank's voice looped in his brain. *'For God's sakes Max – stay out of the shop.'*

Butt Cheeks looked at him, her eyes heavy with expectation.

Naturally, he had no desire to be rude to a customer. *Probably get into trouble for that too. No turning back now.* "Name's Max."

The woman's eyes narrowed, then she spat words at him like shots from a nail gun. "I know who you are."

Max straightened. *Uh-oh. Did a sink hole just open up?* "And…you are?" His sixth sense told him he should probably know the answer to that.

She stepped forward, flung an arm in his direction. "You jerk!"

His eyes flew wide open. "What? I'm sorry love…I-"

"Don't 'love' me." She yelled at him. "I'm not your love."

As if engineered by fate, Frank chose that moment to walk back into the shop – the buzzer went off.

Frank stepped inside the shop. He'd heard yelling as he approached the store. He surveyed the scene – *Max!*

Max read his boss's mind – *"what are you doing in here?"*

Fuck, what was he doing in here?

Frank assessed the angry woman.

Then he looked back at Max. *He could just guess – at it again!*

"Is everything ok here?" Frank plastered a smile on his face.

But Max caught the angry flash in his boss's eyes, and he knew that was for his benefit.

Oh god. He opened his mouth hoping to clear himself with his next words. "Not what it looks like Frankie." Max held up a hand – *innocent.* His other hand clutched the fuel filter close to his body.

Frank reserved his sympathy for the woman. "Is everything ok?" His voice even.

The woman felt her face puff up as a beet-red flush made its way over her cheeks and tracked a course down her neck. She flung both arms down by her side. "No it is definitely not ok."

Frank shot Max an accusatory glare. He spoke through gritted teeth. "What happened?"

"Nothing, I swear." Then Max turned to the woman. "Look, I'm sorry, ok. Whatever it is – I'm sorry Miss…?"

"It's Jenna you jerk!"

Max's heart might have stopped.

Jenna's eyes narrowed to slits. Her lips formed pouts like a puffed up toadfish when it's frightened. She swung her loose hanging, blonde locks for effect.

Now he saw it. *That blonde hair.* He pictured her hair against his chocolate brown lounge cushions. *Oh fuck – Jenna! How did he miss that?*

Jenna swung around on her heel and stormed back down through the aisles, bumping into shelves on her way to the door. The buzzer went off. She let the door swing shut behind her, and clomped along the footpath till she was out of sight.

Max, gob smacked, tried to speak. *Oh fuck.* He felt the full heat of his boss's glare.

The salesman slipped out of the firing line, over to a shelf and started fussing with nothing.

Max shook his head in slow motion as if willing Frank to believe him. "Frank." His tone unmistakably pleading. "Mis…understanding."

No response.

Max felt like he'd waded into a muddy dam boots and all, and his shoes were now being sucked from his feet.

"Frank. It wasn't like that Frank – this has nothing to do with work. This thing with…fuck it!…*Jenna*…was an outside work thing. I promise. I picked her up at a bar." *Not helping.*

The veins on Frank's forehead jiggled as he stood transfixed on Max. He scanned his brain for the right words. But none came. He balled his hands into fists and took a step towards Max.

"Jesus Christ Max! Don't you get it?" Then the walls came crumbling down. "If she comes into this store, she's my customer. By the way…." He pointed to the walls in an almost comical fashion as he yelled. "Workplace! Not your private pick up joint! Then I see…her storm out upset after…you…whatever you did." *Was he making sense?* His face burned hot.

"Calm down Frankie." Max furrowed his brow.

"Don't tell me to calm down!" He took a breath and paused. "What I'm saying is – this has everything to do with work."

"For fuck's sake Frank – will you listen to me."

"Max." His voice a deliberate octave lower. "I'm done listening to you." He ran a hand through his hair, breathed another deep breath and walked behind the counter, past his troublesome employee. "I think it's best if you take some time off Max."

Max's mouth was agape. "What?"

"You heard me."

"Frankie, it was a misunderstanding." He kept his

voice low – the voice of reason.

His boss shook his head. "There seems to be a lot of misunderstandings when it comes to you and women Max."

"Aw come on Frankie. We're friends. You know me."

Frank's eyes widened as he shot Max a knowing glance. *Yes I do.*

"What are you sayin' Frank?" Max shook his head in disbelief. "You don't want me here?"

Frank said nothing.

Max had known his boss a long time, and right now, he guessed he couldn't convince him of anything – least of all his innocence. *He was innocent wasn't he?*

"I can't believe this Frankie." His face slumped. He waited for Frank to change his mind – *sorry Max, heat of the moment. You don't have to go.*

But nothing came.

"Ok then." He placed the part on the counter. He hung his head as he started to walk out the front door. "I'm sorry you feel that way Frankie."

He ambled over to the work shed – looking back at the store as he went. *What just happened?*

The boys in the shed had heard everything.

Rob offered his consolations. "Sorry Max."

"Sucks Max." Kyle shuffled near the tinnie.

"Don't worry about it buddy." Max looked away and shook his head.

He then doled out some quick instructions to Rob so that he could finish off the fuel filter job.

Then he collected his gear.

"See you later Max."

And headed for his truck.

As he closed the door to his truck, the shock of what had just happened started to subside. It was replaced by bruised ego, then mounting injustice. By the time he was turning left out of the carpark and onto the street, the humiliation of it all started to hit home, and then it quickly progressed to full blown anger. He felt the swell inside him.

He watched the reflection of his truck in the windows of the buildings as he drove down the street.

He banged a fist repeatedly into the steering wheel.

Fuck!

***

Gary took a sip from his pot of beer then placed it back down on the bar. He shook his head, barely taking his eyes off the bottles of spirits lined up on the shelves on the back wall of the bar.

"So did he actually fire you?"

Max wrapped his fingers around the foam cooler that held his stubbie. "Good as." He took a swig of his beer.

"I can't believe he would just let you go like that Max. You're too much a part of that place." He knew Max was Frank's best mechanic. "Maybe, if you just talk to him."

Max narrowed his eyes. "You weren't there Baldo. He's not changing his mind." He lifted the stubbie out of the cooler and started to peel off the label, then proceeded to rip it into smaller pieces – his mind replayed the miserable episode. "Too fucking angry at me."

Gary's expression was despondent. "There must be something you can do." He wanted to help – but Max was a hard case.

He'd launched into action the minute he'd heard Max's angry message on his mobile phone – *'I've been fired. I'm gunna get drunk.'*

He knew he wouldn't be too hard to find. He'd left his assistant Paul, in charge of Baldo's Bikes for the rest of the day, and if he didn't come back, then his instructions were to close up at the end of the day. There were only two places Gary knew his mate would likely be holed up at – both of them pubs – and he wasn't at the first one that he'd checked.

On the short drive around the corner to the second pub, a sense of deja vu sent a shiver down his spine – only it wasn't deja vu. It was just the really familiar feeling from *actually* doing this same drive many times before, looking for Max – although the reasons varied.

Flashes of their school days came to mind. Gary had been a tall, awkward kid – and teased frequently because of it. Max had put an end to any future bullying when he'd flattened one of the big kids doing the teasing. *'Fuckin' hate cowards!'* he'd said after he'd done it. Gary smirked. Even then, Max was mean.

It may not have been the right thing to do and today the punishment for doing it would be more severe, but back then, growing up was just rougher somehow – *more like survival.* Hardness was encouraged – applauded even. And Max was hard – even as a kid.

The modern world of 2015 was different to the seventies and eighties influences that marked their early years. The only problem was – while the world had changed, Max had not.

Gary had snapped out of his reverie just in time to make the turn into the carpark behind the second pub. He'd pulled in next to an oceanic blue Colorado truck. *Max.*

Since then, he'd consoled his mate for the best part of the afternoon. The sun had gone down, night had settled in, and by the looks of it, so had Max. He knew he couldn't leave him – he was in for the long haul – until Max stopped feeling sorry for himself, or passed out, whichever happened first. Experience told him it would be the latter.

Gary's eyes now mined for a nugget of hope. "Are you sure there's nothing you can do? Just give him some time to calm down Max, then talk to him again."

His drunken friend raised his stubbie to toast. "Not gonna happen mate." He lifted it higher. "Here's to unemployment." He thumped the glass back down, splashing drops onto the top of the bar. "Fuck. This is just great. I've got a mortgage to pay." He shuddered at the thought. "Fuck!"

The bartender shot a warning look their way. Gary nodded, he understood – keep his mate in line. *But could he?*

"Sorry Baldo." Max wiped his mouth on his shirt sleeve. "You're a good friend hey. Loyalty – that's what it's about." His eyes squinted hard as he thought about what he'd just said. He thought about it as if his life depended on it. "That's all it's fuckin' about!"

Gary shrunk into his stool, and rubbed a sweaty hand across his face.

The pub band that had smashed out its vigorous

sounds for most of the night took a break. Interval music sounded out from the speakers – softer and gentler. The change of pace caused a sombre mood to descend across the entire pub. Max felt it latch onto him, dragging him down further into its depths, ripples of misery expanded out from him.

He felt his eyelids tug. His body grew tired, and his bones suddenly felt like they were made of lead. He closed his eyes for a second, his head started spinning and he allowed the hot, heavy pull of the alcohol to overcome him.

"Max." Gary shook his mate's arm. "Are you ok?"

He jerked up straight. His eyes glazed over.

"Maybe we should get you home Max." It was more of a request than a question.

Max snapped awake. Shook it off. "Forget it mate." He raised his glass again. "I'm not done commis…commish-"

Gary rolled his eyes. "Commiserating."

"That's it." Max pointed a finger.

His mate sighed. *In for the long haul.* He signalled the bartender. "Can we get a plate of potato wedges thanks?" Then as an afterthought he added. "With some sour cream on the side too…and some tomato sauce."

Max bellowed out a crackly laugh. "You really are a pussy Baldo."

"Shut up Max." He reached for the napkins holder, grabbed a handful and plonked a pile on the bar. "You're going to eat something, then I'm taking you home."

Max saluted. "Eye, eye Capt'n."

While they'd been pre-occupied at the bar, they hadn't noticed the number of patrons in the place swell to almost a full house – standing room only.

Gary frowned. *Jesus, it's a Wednesday night.* "Haven't they got anything better to do?" he said to no-one in particular.

The stale smell of alcohol, mixed with the combined stink of body odour and perfumes in the air, made breathing a chore. The chatter in the pub had now become a loud, indistinguishable buzz – an increasingly organic presence – punctuated only by the occasional high pitched squeal or loud whoop. Much of the noise seemed to come from the row of tables along the wall – where groups formed and flourished.

Max spotted a trio of women settled into a corner table. *He hadn't seen them come in.* They were all dressed in suits, clearly straight from work.

Work. Max screwed up his nose.

The women looked like real estate agents. Glossy hair, pulled back tight – their necks trimmed with their little green and yellow bandanas. *How patriotic.*

Gary noticed them too – but more disturbingly, he noticed Max's gaze lock onto them.

"You're not…thinking about going over there?"

Max didn't respond.

"Max?" His voice firmer.

"Of course not." He snapped. But he wasn't convincing. He sneered in the trio's direction. "Look at them giggling and carrying on. Fucking women. They all act so fucking innocent."

"Max." Gary put a steady hand on his mate's shoulder. "They haven't done anything to you. Not all women are like that."

Max shook it off. "Yeah I know. They're not. I know that."

Gary sucked in a relieved breath. The last thing he wanted was for Max to make a scene. They obviously didn't need to make a bad day worse by being kicked out of the pub, or arrested. He knew the real Max, and the real Max loved women. *He was just angry right now. He'll calm down.*

But Max couldn't take his eyes off the women. "Honestly Baldo. Look at 'em. All with their 'come and play with me' looks, then BAM!" He smacked a fist into his hand.

Gary jumped.

"Then they got ya." He continued. "By the short and fuckin' curlys." He twisted his stubbie around and around.

"Ok Max, I think you might have had enough." His voice steady. *Trouble brewing.* "Time to go home. Sleep it off."

But Max was just getting started. "I mean, look at 'em. What the fuck are they giggling at? Women are always giggling." He twisted his face and raised a hand. "I mean, what the fuck is so funny?"

"Hey Max. Stop swearing mate."

Gary glanced at the trio of women. He noticed that one was holding a reading tablet in her lap. Her finger swiping at regular intervals as she skimmed the pages. The other two leaned towards it at irregular intervals, and giggled as they did.

Gary squinted – a memory flashed. He remembered that his ex-girlfriend read 'those' books on a kindle.

She had told him that it was more private that way —
she didn't have to be embarrassed buying the books in
a store.

Gary furrowed his eyebrows. "Probably reading
one of those sex books."

"Jesus Gary, we're in public here." Max snapped his
eyes towards his mate, his voice edged with sarcasm.

The bartender placed their order of potato wedges
in front of them.

"Just eat something Max." He shoved the plate
towards him. "And then I'm gonna get you out of
here."

His reluctant friend picked up the plate of potato
wedges. Shoved one of the oddly shaped pieces in his
mouth.

He held the plate up, and kept his eyes locked onto
the women in the booth. "You know what? I do
believe I'm gonna share these here delicious wedges
with my new friends over there."

Gary's eyes widened. "What?"

But Max was on the move. He was off his stool, on
his feet and tried very hard not to stagger as he walked
over to the women.

Gary bolted off his stool and tugged at his mate's
shirt, trying to pull him back, or at least steer him away.
But his drunken charge had always been stronger than
him.

The determined Max approached the table. The
three women stopped talking instantly and looked up at
him — curious looks on their faces. If any of them were
interested in Max, or thought they'd like to get to know
him better, he put paid to those thoughts as soon as he

opened his mouth to speak.

"Good evening ladies." He chewed with his mouth open, the mashed wedges clearly visible inside. "Why wouldn't you ever starve in a desert?" He fell into the seat next to them.

Gary gripped onto his shirt but it slipped from his hand.

"Because of all the *sand-wedges*." Max erupted with laughter, spitting out bits of potato, and holding out the plate to the women.

The blonde woman spoke first – haughty and firm. "No thanks. We don't want any." But she moved over anyway, because Max was pushing in, like it or not.

"Listen," the redhead said. "Why don't you just go back to your stool over there and leave us alone." She waved a nicely manicured hand. "We don't want you here."

Max's eyebrows shot up. He put a hand across his heart. "That hurts. You know that? Leave you alone hey?"

"Come on Max, let's go. You're drunk." Gary gripped onto his mate's arm and tried to pull him out of the seat.

Max pointed a wavering finger at each of the women. "Let me tell you all…something." He faltered. "You women…don't know what you fucking want. You want a man…you want a pussy-"

Gary cut in. "Ok Max, that's enough." He tried to lift him away from the table, but it was useless – it was like trying to pull up a lump of lead.

"No mate. I'm gonna stay and par-tah with the lah-dies here." He exaggerated his words and held the wedges out in front of him with dramatic flair. Then he shovelled another couple into his mouth in a deliberate attempt to disgust the women.

It worked. They screwed up their faces at him.

He revelled in their disgust – which only encouraged him more. *He was getting a bit of his own back.* He let the chewed up wedges dribble out of his mouth, practically spitting them out on the table and at the women.

"Eww." The women made moves to get out of their seats.

That's right ladies, this is what a real man looks like.

Then in a move that shocked even Gary, and before he could stop him, Max jumped up, and unzipped his pants. "You fucking women suck us guys in…you hear me? You su-uck us in!"

"Well suck on this." Max dropped his pants revealing purple boxers, and wriggled his pelvis around. "I'll show you what a real man looks like. Have you ladies ever seen the Great Eastern One-Eyed Python?"

"Jesus!" Gary tried to stop him.

The women squealed and laughed at Max as they scrambled out of the booth.

But it only spurred him on more.

Gary shook his head. *They're not laughing with you Max.*

The bartender noticed the scene and signalled security.

Max's campaign of harassment ended abruptly when security grabbed him. He wriggled and fought as they escorted him outside.

Gary grabbed their wallets and keys off the bar and scuttled after them. *That was bad. He'd gone too far this time.*

A short drive with a snoring Max in the back seat later, Gary arrived outside of his mate's house.

He shuffled around for his keys, then using himself as a crutch, he managed to get Max to the front door before they stumbled through – the same way Max frequently came through his front door. He got him to the lounge room, peeled off his shoes, and laid a blanket over him.

His inebriated charge came out of his stupor for a brief minute. "Sorry mate."

"Good night Max."

He switched off the light, and shut the front door behind him.

He was sure Max was going to regret this night in the morning.

Chapter Six

Gary rapped his knuckles on Max's front door. He hoped it was annoyingly loud on the inside – enough to wake the hungover Max. He meant business.

He stood waiting for signs of life.

The night before had been humiliating – and not just for Max.

He shivered at the memory – *awful. Jesus Max.*

He knocked again – louder. His face determined. He ran a hand through his light brown hair. He was taking charge of things today. *Not always an easy thing to do with Max.*

Yesterday was terrible. He felt sympathy for his mate – he really did. Things had been looking up for Max lately and yes the work situation sucked. No doubt about it. But last night at the pub – *Max brought that on himself.*

And further, he planned to remind Max at an opportune moment, that last night was not a good look for the new coach of the under tens junior football.

Max often seemed to have problems with women –

somehow just attracted it. He'd seen it with almost all of his girlfriends – not that he'd that many – and never for that long. One in particular, Susan, a particularly bright and enthusiastic girl had hung in the longest – at least six months. But inevitably, that also crashed and burned. *"What did I do?"* Max had asked at the time, completely dumfounded. *"I thought we were gettin' on ok."*

Gary shifted from one foot to the other, flicking his thongs against the cement floor of Max's front porch. *Still no sound.* There may not have been any sign of life inside, but he knew Max was in there. And he knew he would be hungover – *and feeling sorry for himself.*

He knocked again, this time with more force.

As he waited, his own failed relationships flashed to mind. They may not have been as fiery as Max's, but they were passable, and a couple even long term. They just didn't work out for one reason or another. It didn't stop him from trying though. Unlike, Max, Gary wanted to find a girl and settle down – get married, have some kids.

He paced back and forth. *Where is Max?*

He stepped off the porch and walked around to the side of the house till he reached Max's bedroom window. He banged on the rippled glass.

"Max!"

He heard a soft thump. "Alright alright already…I'm up!" Max's voice was tired and gravelly. "Stop banging will you."

Gary scooted back to the front door – grinning. He heard shuffling noises as Max staggered down the hall towards the front door. *Serves you right Max.* He cared – he did – he just wasn't impressed.

Max swung open the door. "Where's the fucking fire?"

He looked bad. Still in his work clothes, crumpled and minus his shoes, he was unkempt, unshaven, and stank of sweat and alcohol – his hair, a rat's nest.

"You look like shit Max." A gust of Max's smell wafted over him. "And you stink something shocking hey."

"Baldo," Max said, still holding the door. "Nice to see you too." He let go of the door, turned and shuffled back down the hall.

"Oh no you don't!" Gary swung the door shut behind him. "This way." He pointed to the kitchen.

Max turned and sneered as he locked eyes with his mate. "What?"

"You heard me. Kitchen. Coffee. Now."

"You think you're here to rescue me Baldo?"

Gary stood tall. "As a matter of fact Max, yes I am."

Max ignored him, and turned back towards his bedroom.

His mate's tone was firm. "Max!" He stamped his foot.

Max swung around, his eyes narrowed. "Did you just stamp your foot at me like a girl?"

Gary's eyes darted left then right. "I might've. Hard to say."

Then suddenly, Max burst out a crackly laugh.

"I don't see what's so funny Max."

Max waved an arm at him. "I'm sorry Baldo. It's just when you act all serious like that, it's hilarious. What are we – back in primary school?"

Yes well. "Glad to be fodder for your amusement Max."

He squeezed out every last remnant of his laugh, then wiped his eyes. "God that was good. Thanks Baldo – that's just what I needed. You're a real woman Baldo – you know that?"

"You're a real idiot Max – you know that?" Then he pointed to the kitchen.

"What's the big plan here Baldo? You gonna bawl me out over coffee?"

"No. I'm not." His voice calm again – *and hopefully in charge.* "I'm taking you out in the boat today."

Max's eyebrows shot up, his eyes wide. "Really?"

"Yes really."

"It's Thursday.   Don't you wanna wait till the weekend?"

They often went out fishing in Max's boat – on weekends. It was a local pastime.

Gary stood his ground firmly in the hallway. "Well the last time I checked, you don't have a job to go to."

Max glared at him.   "Bit harsh isn't it?" He scratched his goatee. "What about your shop?"

"Got Paul to look after it today. I can take a day off you know."

"Got it all planned out then haven't you?" He felt like shit. The last thing he wanted to do was go out – anywhere. Wallowing at home seemed like a much better plan.

"Yep."   Gary nodded with enthusiasm.   "Boat's fuelled and hooked up to my ute – out front – all ready to go." He pointed towards the front door.

Max peered out the front and saw his boat hooked

up to Gary's old banger of a ute. They used Gary's ute to save Max's Colorado from getting knocked around and wrecked by the salt-water while it was still so new.

"I've checked the safety gear, checked the fuel – all good to go."

Max pointed a finger. "You know Baldo, I gotta get that shed key back from you."

His mate rolled his eyes. "You're an idiot Max." He brushed past him and strolled into the kitchen like he owned the place.

"So you keep saying." He followed.

"Are you mad at me Baldo? 'Cause I'm sensing some agro here."

"Not at all. I love being humiliated in front of half the town."

Max's face flashed guilty. "Ok." He plonked down on a stool at his small island bench. "Coffee would be good."

"Still two sugars and milk?" Gary reached into the cupboard under the benchtop and pulled out two mugs. *Which reminded him.* "Got some food and drink to take with us too." His expression suddenly stern. "Just water and coffee."

"We're going on a picnic?" Max mocked. "You're such a pussy Baldo."

"It's not a picnic. Don't be a prick." He folded his arms.

"Ok, ok." He surrendered. "Seems like I don't have a choice."

"You always have a choice Max." His statement weighed heavy. "But I'm not going to let you sit here and wallow all day."

Max nodded as he felt the pang of guilt deepen. *Could always rely on his mate.* A tiny crack formed in his hard exterior. He shook it off, cleared his throat and got a grip. If he wasn't careful, the swell of emotions he'd been holding at bay would find the crack and burst through. But then last night flashed to mind – *possibly already did.*

"Guess you got me home last night." His smile was sheepish.

"Guess so."

"And my truck?"

"Uh-huh."

"Thanks."

Gary nodded, then flicked on the kettle as he reached for the jar of instant coffee Max kept on the sink. He grabbed a teaspoon out of the drawer and scooped a spoon of coffee into each mug.

Max sat and stared out at nothing. The swell was heading for the crack again, trickling out. He shook his head. *God what had happened over the past twenty-four hours?*

He recounted – got the shock of his life over Jenna, got humiliated, got fired, got kicked out of the pub – for being an arse. *Ok, he deserved that last one.*

"What a fucking mess." He shoved his face in his hands, then ran both hands over the top of his head.

"Guess so." His friend poured the water, then milk into the mugs – added Max's sugar. "You hungry?" He pointed to the fridge.

Max shook his head, the bitter aftertaste of a bad night still in his mind, in his gut. He could taste the stale beer in his mouth. "No. Not really."

The trickle burst through. He thumped a fist down

onto the bench. "What a fuck-up! What am I supposed to do now Baldo?"

Gary placed a mug of coffee in front of him. "I'll tell you want you are going to do now." He shoved the mug closer. "You are going to drink this." His look was serious. "Then go get yourself cleaned up – you really stink hey – get your fishing gear on." He pointed to his own shorts and t-shirt. "Then we're going out on the boat. High tide's at eight o'clock – a.m."

Max glanced up and smirked. "Yeah ok – whatever. I suppose I got nothin' better to do." *Probably would be a good distraction. Clear his head. Fuck he felt like a loser.*

"Guess they won't be letting us back into the pub for a while huh?" His smile was forced.

His mate returned the gesture. "I don't think so Max."

***

It was still early morning by the time they arrived at the boat ramp. They'd driven twenty minutes to the popular boating and fishing community of Boonooroo.

"Baldo, you drive like a girl. Move it will you."

"Shut up Max. I gotta go careful – boat's on the back."

It was a Thursday, so they didn't expect many people on the water. They pulled into the bush car park that led down to the boat ramp.

Max breathed a sigh of relief. *No-one else here.*

On a Saturday, this area would be full and they'd have to wait their turn. But not today.

"Good." Max smiled. It also meant he wouldn't have to face anyone if word had gotten out about his terrible behaviour at the pub last night. He lived in a small town but the Boonooroo community was even smaller.

He glanced out at the water. A long pontoon floated alongside the boat ramp.

Gary lined the ute and trailer up, ready to reverse it down into the water.

"Want me to do it?" Max offered.

"Nope I'm good."

"Come on Baldo, you know you suck at reversing. I'm better at. Let me do it."

"Shut up Max, I'm trying to concentrate."

He eased the trailer down the ramp, submerging it until the water was just under the wheel bearings. He yanked on the handbrake and cut the engine.

They made quick work of shoving the boat off the trailer and tying it up to a stainless steel cleat on the pontoon. Gary tossed the fishing gear, esky and flask into the tinnie.

Max babysat the boat while his mate parked the ute and empty trailer under a tree. As he waited, he breathed in the salt water air. It really was a beautiful morning. Even Max could appreciate that. The air was still cool, but a warmth was beginning to bite and he knew it wouldn't be long until the summer sun poured its sticky heat into it. They'd suffered one heatwave after another this summer and the forecast predicted more to come.

Can't believe he lost his job. He forced the thought away, and let the rhythm of the water slapping against the boat, soothe him.

"Max!"

His reverie broken – he looked up to see Gary staring down at him from the pontoon. His mate climbed over the side of the boat, planting his feet with a thud on the floor.

"A little respect for the boat will ya." He frowned.

"Sorry."

Max turned the key to start the seventy horsepower, two stroke outboard motor. He stood ready with his hands on the steering wheel.

"Forget it mate." Gary's tone was firm. "You'll still be over the limit for driving the boat. I'm driving."

"Baldo, you drive this boat like you drive your ute." He teased. "Like you're driving Miss Daisy."

"Well if you hadn't drank so much last night, we'd be driving your preferred way instead – like a madman possessed." He shoved Max out of the way and gripped the wheel. Then he added. "Your actions have consequences."

Max sniffed loudly for effect. *Indeed they do.*

"Now untie that rope for me."

Max did as he asked. He let Baldo get away with talking to him in a way that others wouldn't dare. In his heyday, Max'd had a reputation for being a bit wild and unpredictable – lots of fights and drunken brawls. And he'd dragged Baldo into most of them. But his friend wasn't a fighter – far from it.

They idled out of the mouth of the creek, which was nestled behind a row of mangrove trees. They stayed under the speed limit – six knots – it was slow, but law, until they cleared the many boats moored in the creek.

As they reached the navigation markers that led out into the deep water, Gary thrust the throttle forward to put the revs on.

Max gripped the side handle on the centre console to hold on. He frowned at his mate.

They reached a cruising speed of twenty knots. Gary trimmed the outboard and the boat travelled smoothly along the top of the water.

Max glanced back – white water trailed out from behind the propeller.

They weaved around the navigation markers that indicated where the deep water was – green to red, red to green on the way out of the channel.

The wind whipped their faces. The tinnie's sides were high and held back most of the spray, but when it hit, the salt water stung their eyes.

Max smiled. He was alive again.

Gary laughed out loud. *Yep, right thing to do.* He kept a good lookout, to avoid any turtles and other sea animals in the tinnie's path, as well as any crab pot floats where they shouldn't be. He took a breath of the salt water air. Then peered out onto the horizon – the deep water looked like it had been laid with a blanket of blue velvet. The sun sparkled down on the smooth waves, dancing diamonds across the water. He could hear Max's voice in his head. *'Baldo, you're a woman."* He enjoyed the view anyway.

Max pointed to a land mass up ahead. "We can pull up at the Reef Islands just before Fraser Island." He had to yell over the roar of the engine and the wind in their ears.

"How long?" Gary asked.

"Fifteen minutes."

As they approached the tiny, uninhabited Reef

Islands, which were really just mud banks saturated with mangrove trees, Gary dropped the revs back – too fast. They held on tight, feet planted on the deck. As the boat ripped back to a stop, the water propelled past them, the swell knocking the boat as if it'd been hit by a wave.

Their hearing returned.

"Fuck you're rough on the wheel Baldo. I'm driving back."

Gary shook his head and grinned. "Just tell me where you want me to pull up."

"Turn off the engine." He barked out the order. "We can drift along the edge of the oyster bank here." It was one of his favourite fishing spots.

Gary cut the engine.

Quiet rushed back in – the air still and silent, as if they'd been yelling at a club and the music stopped.

Max inhaled the salt air. *Freedom!* Immediately, he felt his body relax. *God he loved the water.* He smiled – and this time, it felt real.

His mate tossed him a packet of worms.

They baited their fishing lines and cast them out. Gary slotted his in a pole holder on the edge of the boat and reached for the flask of coffee.

"Keep the noise down will ya Baldo – you'll scare the fish away."

The tinnie was a floating tin can with the engine turned off. The water slapped the aluminium hull. They were in the shallows – enough to see the rocky, shaley bottom of the ocean floor.

"What do ya reckon we'll catch here?" Gary asked.

"Whiting. Maybe some bream."

"Ok, good." He nodded.

Hours disintegrated as they sat, fished, ate and drank coffee in virtual silence.

"You were right Baldo," Max said. "This is exactly what I needed today."

His mate smiled.

"I dunno what I'm gonna do mate." He breathed out a heavy sigh. "I've gotta pay my mortgage, my car. Lucky the boat's paid for."

"I know mate." He tossed him another packet of worms.

"Not a lot of jobs around town."

"What about 'Southern Outboards'?"

Max shook his head. "Nah mate. They're doin' it tough. I doubt they can afford another mechanic."

Gary thought for a minute. "What about down the bay?" *Hervey Bay.*

"Maybe." Max grinned. "Do ya think Frankie would give me a reference?"

He frowned. "Maybe a bit too soon."

Max nodded. *Maybe.*

Images of last night's events flashed back to him. *The women in the bar.* He shook his head. "Pretty bad wasn't it? I made a real arse of myself."

"You did." He couldn't disagree.

He rolled his eyes. "Thanks for the support."

"Well what do you want me to say mate. You behaved like a fucking moron."

Max nodded. "I did, didn't I?" Then a thought struck him. "Did you know any of those women?"

"At the table?"

Max nodded.

"The ones that you spat food all over and tried to flash your big fella at?"

Max felt the heat in his cheeks rise. "Fuck me. What did I do?"

"No." Gary admitted. "I didn't recognise any of 'em." Then as an afterthought or to be funny, he wasn't sure. "And no, I don't think any of them would go out with you after that performance."

"Not what I was thinking Baldo." He shook his head. "Fuck. What a prick I was."

His mate raised his eyebrows in response. *Not arguing with that.*

"I was just so angry mate, after being kicked like that by Frank."

"I know. It sucked." He didn't have to say the rest – *it didn't excuse your behaviour.* Yet he felt compelled to add. "Those women didn't do anything to you, you know. They were just minding their own business – probably after work drinks, reading and just generally being women."

Max sneered. "Yeah, just being women." But a thought crossed his mind. "They were reading something weren't they?"

"Aw, think so." *Where was he going with this?*

"Hey Baldo, what did ya say they were readin'?"

"I dunno." He fussed with his fishing pole – thought he felt a tug.

"No, seriously. What was it you said to me last night about what they were reading?"

"I dunno Max. I think, maybe that sex stuff for women." He shook his head at his friend, distracted by the slack line again. He sat back down. "You've been living under a rock."

He could see the curiosity in his friend's face.

"The mummy porn stuff. Remember, I tried to tell you about it? You know, the sicko stuff for women."

Max screwed up his face.

He backtracked. "Well I don't think it's all sicko stuff. Some of it's just regular sex I think." His face flushed red. *Embarrassing.*

"Are you blushing Baldo?"

"No, of course not." He talked quickly. "I don't know. Tanya used to read it. Wanted us to-" But he stopped himself.

"What?" Max straightened on his seat, alert. Now he was definitely interested. "She like the kinky stuff did she?" He flashed a sly grin.

"No!" Gary's blush wouldn't go down. "It's not all kinky. Some of it's just regular sex stuff."

"So you keep sayin'. Sounds like you know more than ya letting on Baldo." He winked.

He shook his head. "Well, anyway." He feigned intense interest in his fishing line. "Apparently, it's a big thing now. Women love it. Tanya reckons some people have made a lot of money out of it."

Max looked confused.

"Writing it." He explained.

Max rubbed his chin. "So they write about sex and woman buy it?"

"I guess."

Then Gary saw the cogs turning in his mate's head. "Max you're not...? Thinking...."

"Why not?" He chewed on the thought with more serious intent.

"Max, what do you know about writing?"

"I can write."

"Since when?" His eyes popped.

"I got a computer – can type a bit." *There was that one semester of typing they made the boys take in high school.* "And I definitely know about having sex with women."

Gary laughed. "What? You barely made it out of high school!" His eyes wide. "And I'm not sure you know the right things about women."

"I'm a man ain't I?"

Gary nodded slowly. *That might be the problem Max.* "You don't know the first thing about what women want to read…or romance for that matter, or what kind of a man they want – or any kind of stuff like that."

"You know what Baldo?" Max jabbed the air repeatedly with his index finger. "Neither do they."

His mate rolled his eyes.

"It's true mate. Women are all, 'come here', 'go away', 'touch this', 'don't touch that', 'please that'." He continued his little tirade. "They want a man, but they date pussies. All new-age sensitive men, then they're genuinely surprised when they can't fucking do anything for them."

Gary had nothing.

"You know what the secret to what a women wants is?" Max leaned in, as if he had the answer to the mystery of life itself.

"Pray tell me please oh love guru."

"They want a real man – one that they can depend on when the shit goes down. They just don't fucking know it!" He practically bounced in his folding chair.

"They think they gotta own you and tell you want to do, but what they really want is for the man to take charge – take control – tell *them* what to do."

I'm not sure that's quite right Max. But Gary had heard enough.

"Ok, enough talk of women." He tossed another packet of bait at him. "We're here to fish. Settle down." Then he grinned.

They spent the rest of the morning fishing, laughing, telling jokes and by the time the midday heat started to beat down unbearably, they decided to call it quits for the day – and Max was a changed person.

Yes a definite positive outlook had crept over him – as a germ of an idea had taken hold.

***

Max sat at his computer. *Ok, a bit of research first.*

He sat attentive, and tapped into the keyboard. It was slow, but he was grateful for that semester of typing in high school that they made the boys do.

What is mummy porn? He typed it slowly into his search engine. His first hits came back quickly.

A dictionary definition flashed up at him:

> "Novels… written for women and contain sexual themes and descriptions."

"Huh. Sexual themes and descriptions." He muttered to himself. He read on:

> "…new genre of novels…erotic scenes…designed to appeal to readers who are middle-aged women…descriptions and visual

pictures intended to give sexual excitement…"

"Not seeing a problem here. I've given women plenty of sexual excitement." He told the wall. He wondered why more men hadn't cottoned on to the idea of writing erotica novels.

He checked another hit on his computer. The word 'dominating' appeared more than once. *That's right. Women like the man to take charge. Got it!*

And that was it. Max had read all he needed to know about writing erotica novels. He thought about what kind of story he might write. He'd read somewhere that you should always write what you know. *That makes sense.*

He'd do that. He'd spent plenty of time in bars and clubs. He'd picked up a few women in his time and even brought a couple or more home. Feeling pretty satisfied that he had some material to start with, he decided to write about his own experiences with women – *maybe embellish them a little.*

He recalled his conversation with Baldo earlier that day on the boat. *"Women want a real man,"* he'd told Baldo. *"One that takes charge."*

And that's exactly what he would give them!

Chapter Seven

Katherine Wilkins banged her front door shut behind her. She launched into a jog, hurtling the small shrubs near her letterbox, cutting across to the footpath.

Then she settled into a steady pace. She heard her sneakers scrape the cement each time her feet hit the ground. She thought of Sal. *Yes she did wear them on her weekend jogs.*

"Good morning Katherine." A fellow jogger waved.

Her eyes flicked wide with surprise. "Oh hi Annie." But she didn't stop. She tracked along the same route out of the estate that she and Sally followed to the bus stop on weekdays, except this time, she turned right at the massive stone entrance, crossed over the main road and headed towards a high school on the other side.

She puffed out hot, heavy breaths. She put on the pace, pushing herself hard, and even though the morning was still young, she could feel the heat starting to chase away any cool left in the air. She mentally calculated her jog. *Forty-five minutes at her desired speed.*

She had needed this jog alone today. Her mind was a stranglehold of doubts. *Thanks to Sally.*

She knew she'd rendezvous with her housemate soon, when Sally 'dropped off' her jogging companions. Katherine smirked. *Jogging companions my arse.* Sal and her cohorts chatted, socialised and generally fluffed about for the entire jog. *More like a leisurely social stroll.*

Sally really did have a different take on life – and it was her different views on men that had really rattled Katherine the other day. All that banging on about 'nice' men and – *safe and boring Steven.*

In one foul swoop – or maybe it'd been a series of smaller swoops – her friend had upset Katherine's well rooted ideas of what she wanted in a man. It was as if a switch had changed the channel in her brain – and a different program was playing – one she'd never seen before – called 'What Katherine Really Wants in a Man'.

Her whole life, she'd used a well-worn checklist that she mentally ticked off when she met a man – *professional, educated, well dressed, well groomed, well spoken, no swearing, polite and courteous.* It seemed like the full package. *Didn't it?* Ok, she admitted there wasn't much room for error. *So what? Why shouldn't she aim high? Right?*

She'd never questioned her stringent criteria for choosing a man before. *So why was she doing it now? What's changed?*

She huffed, and searched for the answers within herself, but all she found was uncertainty and confusion. It etched across her face, setting her expression into a frown for most of her jog. *Was Sally right? Did her checklist really result in a boring man?* Steven had ticked all her boxes. *Was Steven boring?* Then a revolutionary question took root in her brain. *Could she ever be happy with boring?*

Her pace now pounding – she hoped to outrun the whirlwind of thoughts in her head.

Her snug shorts and loose fitting t-shirt were wet with perspiration. She'd pinned up her trademark ponytail into a loose bun, so that it wouldn't stick to her neck as she jogged.

Finally she pulled her speed back, and settled into an easier pace. She forced her mind to focus on happier thoughts – *the past few weeks at work were good.* Her clients were happy, which meant her bosses were happy. They sold a good product – a solid platform for their clients' works – and she was a star at increasing sales revenues.

She smiled – satisfied and proud – as she thought of her achievements at work. This was something she *could* control – and she loved hitting the mark of what she set out to do.

She also mentally patted herself on the back for almost reaching her target for a deposit on her first house. A twinge of excitement ran through her at the thought. *Her own home.*

Then the frown came back. *So what was missing?*

She unhooked the small water bottle that she kept clipped to the waist of her shorts and sipped it without breaking stride.

Right – a man.

The thoughts flooded back. *God, she'd really thought she'd had that all worked out.* A stab of urgency needled its way into her subconscious. She was thirty-two – reality check. *Should she be worried?*

Sally's words churned in her mind. *"You need more excitement in your life…perfect's not out there Kat, it's just real messy."*

She shook her head. *Could the flippant, high-octane Sally know more about this than she did?*

"Excitement…really." She muttered.

How could she plan a solid future if all she was chasing was excitement?

Her feet beat down on the pavement again. Doubts pecked at her – like a woodpecker had taken up residence in her head. *Turmoil! She couldn't make plans based on turmoil.*

Thoughts thrashed around inside her.

Pretty soon, she was a sticky, overheated mess. Then she saw the culprit responsible for her current dilemma up ahead. The distinctive bobbing of Sally's short, blonde ponytail took on a life of its own. Sal was on her own again, clearly having 'dropped off' her jogging party.

Sally waved, a big smile erupting across her face. "Hi Kat!" Her voice an octave above necessary.

Katherine waved and smiled back. Sally was only a couple years younger than herself, but sometimes it felt like they were poles apart. *"You're so serious,"* Sally often said to her. *"Lighten up."*

Maybe Sally was right. Maybe Sal's bubble and light outlook on life was better than her own conservative ways.

She could see her friend clearer now as she drew closer – her fair skin contrasted with her fluorescent orange shorts and yellow tank top – *hope she's wearing sunblock.*

Katherine glanced down at her own arms – her olive skin tanned rather than burned.

Her friend closed the distance in a juvenile sprint. "Hi Kat. How're you going?"

"Pretty good." She smiled. It was hard to be angry at someone with such effervescence.

"Cleared your mind yet?" She winked.

"Yeah." Then she shook her head. "No, not really."

Her friend's face slumped.

Katherine turned and started the jog back home.

Sal followed.

"How were the others?" She changed the subject.

"Good." Sally's breaths blew out ragged as she tried to talk and jog at the same time.

Katherine grinned. *That's what you get for not training properly.*

"They were all buzzing about the new release of…you know…that book."

Katherine's eyes shot to the ground. *No I don't know.*

"You know the one?"

No I really don't.

Sally's voice was suddenly high. "Katherine Wilkins! Don't pretend you don't know."

Katherine's eyes grew wide with shock. "What? I…."

Sal smirked. "Aw come on Kat, I know you read

those books."

"What? How do you know that?" She took the bait.

Sally's eyes ballooned, she turned and ran backwards so she could see her friend's face. "What? I didn't…not for sure!" She stared at her housemate, her voice excited. "Not till just then…I was just teasing you."

"Oh god." Katherine hung her head and almost came to a stop.

Sal put a hand on her arm and giggled. "It's nothing to be ashamed of. I'm proud of you."

"Proud of me? Why?"

"For stepping outside your comfort zone." She was back by her side again. "There's nothing wrong with reading them. They're meant for women – for women's enjoyment."

The world went silent. Seconds felt like hours.

Sally raised an eyebrow. "So? What do you think?"

"What do you mean?"

"Well do you have any fantasies like that?"

"God no!" She picked up the pace again.

Sally kept abreast of her, laughing. "Kat don't be such a prude. Even *you* are only human."

The heat rose in Katherine's face – every pore was on fire with embarrassment.

"Kat?" Sally narrowed her eyes, her voice lowered. "You do don't you? Fantasise?"

Katherine couldn't stop the smile that spread across her face. But she immediately shook it away. "I'm not discussing this."

"Ok. That's fine." She flung her hands in the air.

"Well do you want to hear about mine?"

The answer was quick. "No, Sal!" A shocked little laugh escaped her lips, as she pounded the ground harder. Her voice dropped to barely a whisper. "I don't want to know about your sexual fantasies."

Her friend burst out a loud laugh. "Ok." She sped up to catch her. "We'll talk about something else then." She paused. "How's Steven?"

Katherine grinned.

"What's that grin for?"

She admitted. "Ok, you might have been right about Steven."

"Hallelujah!"

Katherine rolled her eyes. "It's just…well he ticked all my boxes ok."

"You and your frickin' boxes!"

She pulled her lips into a straight line. *Yes well.*

"You going to tell him?"

"Who?"

"Steven." She waved a hand in the air.

"Probably." She blew out a heavy sigh. "We have a date planned for next Friday night. I guess I'll talk to him then."

"Sucks."

"Yeah."

They jogged along for a few more silent seconds – their house up ahead. Katherine suddenly stopped, then turned to face her friend straight on, a wistful look in her eyes.

"Sal, what if I've had the boxes all wrong?" She shook her head as she dwelled on the thought. "I mean, are there other qualities in a man that I should've been looking for…or should be looking for? I don't know what to think anymore."

Sally's eyes grew wide. *She's asking me for advice?* "Well." She nodded. "I for one think so."

"Well what else do you think I should be looking for?" She put her hands on her hips and doubled over to catch a breath.

"Well you must be confused if you've finally resorted to asking me." She rested a hand on her friend's shoulder. "Honey, only you can really answer that question. It's different for every woman."

Katherine shook her head. *Not the advice she was hoping to get.* "I don't know. I guess…no it sounds silly."

"Tell me."

"Well…I suppose, I just want to be…inspired."

Sally raised an eyebrow. "By a man?"

"Yeah."

Uncharacteristically, Sally said nothing.

But Katherine had opened the flood gates. "I like a man to be sensitive, or at least I think so. But I want something more. Not controlling of course, but just…strong you know."

Yes she did know. "So he can protect his woman." Sal mocked and flicked her friend's ponytail.

"Do you think?" Her tone now more desperate than she was used to.

"Of course honey. It's started in the caveman days."

Her eyes narrowed. "I prefer someone a little more refined than that."

"So let me sum it up." She counted on her fingers.

"You want a strong man — but refined, capable and smart, but not controlling or overbearing, sensitive but still able to protect you."

"I…guess."

"It's a hard list honey." She tilted her head at her friend. "Sounds like you want two different guys." She gave her a quick squeeze around the shoulders, then darted ahead towards their house. "Come on. I'll race you home!"

But Katherine was slow to catch up — her thoughts immobilised her. She'd hoped that finally voicing them would help. But somehow saying them out loud had only made them more real. She squinted into the distance.

Are you sure you even know what you want Kat?

Chapter Eight

Max sat in a heightened state of readiness – chair pulled in snug to the kitchen table, laptop in front of him, fingers hovering above the keyboard, word document open and cursor flashing. Then he slowly tapped out a few more words.

"This isn't so difficult." He muttered, then chuckled to himself. He'd been writing his erotica novel for the best part of a week now. He'd wasted no time – jumped straight into it after his day out on the water with Baldo. *When you're onto a good thing.*

He tapped out another sentence, hit the full stop button and smiled. His story was almost complete. It may not have been very long, but what it lacked in length, it made up for in content. *Yep it was good.* He was certain of it. He put some finishing touches on one of his favourite scenes. Then skimmed it again, proud as punch.

He leaned back in his chair, arms stretched upwards, admiring his work. *Awesome.* With a mischievous grin and crazy eyes, feeling like one of those accountants in the television ads when they find some obscure deduction, he read back over his work again, delighted with the results. He jiggled the mouse. *Yes. Yes. Yes.*

"Women are gonna love this."

He thought about the main character that he'd created. He had put a lot of consideration into what type of man he should be, but in the end decided to model his character on how *he* thought a *real man* should be. *That's what women really want. A real man. Not a pussy.*

He had cobbled together some scenes based on his own experiences at clubs, but enhanced the experiences, making them…*more manly*. He read over his favourite scene again.

'Rock cruised into the club. He stopped at the entrance to survey the scene. The light was dull and the air, lifeless and thick with heat. But he didn't care. He had come here for one purpose, and one purpose only – to select a lucky woman to come home with him and fuck all night. He needed it – hungered for it. His insides were raging and he needed the release.

He scanned his eyes around the club, like the terminator, paying particular attention to the bar tables dotted around the dancefloor, trying to lock onto a target. The tables were sparse of clubbers – particularly female clubbers. *Pickings were slim.*

The split level club reminded him of the stands at a football match. He liked football. He cast his eyes upwards to search the level above. *A few possibles – he'd need a better look.*

Almost an hour went by. He wandered the club –

he was a bitch in heat – or rather, the dog that could smell the bitch in heat. He changed tables – frequently. Always looking for a better angle, a better spot, a better woman. He spread himself around, endearing himself to the occasional clubber. Some were regulars, some were hags – he quickly ruled them out. None passed the test.

He was on a mission – he was looking for something fresh. He sighed. So far tonight, all he was doing was wading through a sea of dogs and ugly chicks. *Where are the hot girls?*

Then, as if the gods were smiling down on him and had heard his prayers, he spied a hot chick up ahead. *Hot chick alert!*

She was leaning over a rail – arse barely covered by her tiny black skirt – talking to someone he couldn't see up on the next level.

He honed in on her – *target locked* – and closed the distance between them with predatory speed. Then as he reached his mark, he administered the standard greeting given by all self-respecting horny men – and slapped her on the arse.

She spun around in a fit of surprise and shock.

He extended his hand. "I'm Rock."

He watched her face contort into a grimace. *Probably can't believe her luck.*

"What?" Her expression was strained, confused.

Then he remembered the line he'd rehearsed. "Sorry. Name's 'Hard'. 'Rock Hard'."

"Is that some kind of a joke?" She stood up straight, thrust her chest out.

Yep she liked what she saw too.

"I never joke with the ladies."

"Does that line work for you?"

"Yes. Usually."

"I find that hard to believe."

"Well you might find the size of my cock hard to believe too."

He pretended to unzip his trousers and flash her a preview. He knew that's all that he needed to do – and all that she needed to know. Women liked big dicks. It was a fact of life. They act all prim and proper and offended, but in the end, it's about the big dick. And Rock Hard's dick was big.'

Max chuckled away to himself as he read over that last bit. *Yeah that's good.* He remembered his research about mummy porn. "Sexual themes and descriptions. Check." He consulted his research notes and read them out loud. "Visual pictures intended to give sexual excitement. Check."

Yep. All there. That will definitely sell.

He decided to start writing the 'love scene' next. Rock Hard was bringing the woman from the club home and he was planning some serious action.

For inspiration, Max thought back to his night with Jenna, *the girl from the RSL – and the one that got him fired.* He remembered Jenna's reaction when she saw him in his full glory, ready to please her. He thought about how it had excited him too and spurred him on.

He realised he was lacking certain technical descriptions – he figured he'd need these to make the scenes – *a bit more realistic.* Damn it, he couldn't see a way around it. He was going to have to get into the nitty gritty of writing about men and women's 'sex bits' in his story. *Hmm….*

He hadn't actually read a mummy porn book – or any form of erotica book for that matter. So the only thing he had to draw on was his own experience with women. *Had he paid enough attention?* He tried to visualise Jenna and other women he'd been with. He realised the lights were usually low and in any case – *no he hadn't paid that much attention.*

Of course he had the basics down. He knew there was a vagina, clitoris and some magic spot called 'G'. And that it all sort of worked together. He supposed he could fudge it a bit. He knew enough about the man's bit of course, having one of his own. He'd concentrate on that, confident that he could easily describe Rock Hard's penis in the love scene. An unexpected moment of weirdness flashed over him. *Thinking about another man's penis.* He shivered.

He scurried off to the bathroom and after a few minutes of semi-nakedness and a mirror, he came up with a list of realistic descriptors that he thought he'd be able to use.

He tapped out a draft sex scene, snickering all the while. Then pretty happy with his work, he read over it again.

'Rock ushered Tara into his den. It was a cold winter's night and he'd had the foresight to start a fire in the hearth before he'd left to cruise the clubs.

He had convinced Tara that he wasn't the sicko pervert that she first took him for at the club, and that he could show her a good time. "A real good time," he'd said with a wink intended to further reinforce the message that he meant to do that with his big penis.

He'd bought her a drink and asked her about her interests. "Do you like whales?" he'd asked.

"Yes." She'd replied with a smile, glad he'd taken an interest.

"Well there's a hump back at my place."

She'd rolled her eyes, but her infectious laugh told him that yes, she wanted him too.

Rock's den was spacious, with a set of soft, black, leather modular lounges set against the outer two walls. A smart set of three paintings – all matching – hung on the wall above one of the lounges.

"Classy." Tara noted.

A fireplace was the centrepiece on the back wall as they walked into the room.

Tara's eyes were wide. "Wow, romantic."

Rock reached for a super soft blanket from a nearby chair and spread it out on the floor, just close enough to the warmth of the fire. He snatched a handful of coloured potpourri out of a nearby table ornament that was left behind by a previous girlfriend, and flung it out over the blanket. He smiled. *Nice touch.*

Then with a sweep of his hand he invited. "Madam." His voice smooth and kind.

He removed his cream jacket, exposing a multi-coloured shirt underneath, neatly tucked into matching cream pants. *His club gear.*

Tara watched Rock as he easily moved around the room. He was an attractive man. No doubt. Sandy hair, swept neat, green eyes, solid frame, pretty tall. *Yes, he definitely had the goods.* He'd really made an effort over the next couple hours after that initial butt slap. She saw the real Rock.

She thought it was nice how he'd made an effort to meet her girlfriends. He'd even cooed with appreciation when she showed him a photo from her purse of her new pet pussy, "Ralph".

No, he didn't seem so bad. He had also invited her friends back to his house – *thoughtful* – but ultimately, she had decided to go alone. He seemed trustworthy enough, her friends knew where she was – they were just a phone call away. Besides, she was horny – and he promised her a big penis. She thought about that now and tracked his movements with lust in her eyes. He was a desirable man – *with a big penis.*

"Wine?" Rock thrust a glass of red in front of her, breaking her daydream.

"Oh." She took the glass.

He clinked it against his own – his smile bearing down on her.

Rock moved his eyes over the woman in front of him. *What a peach.* She looked like a whore in her short, shiny dress – tied around her neck with a bow. Her blonde hair cascaded down over her shoulders – those sexy shoulders. *Fuck she was hot.* He'd worked her all night at the club – and now here she was. *Ripe for the picking.*

He knew he had to take charge now. He was the man. It was his job. *The man should take the lead – take control.* Then the woman would follow. He knew she wanted that and he wasn't planning to disappoint. *They all secretly loved to be dominated.* But he had to time it right.

"Kneel down," he told her. *No time like the present.*

"What?" Her voice a squeak.

"You heard me." He lowered his glass to a small side table. His voice firm. "Kneel. Down."

She giggled. *Where is this going?* But she played along. She slowly kneeled down on the super soft blanket, being careful not to stick the heels of her shoes into it.

Rock stepped towards her until he stood right in front of her, hovering over her head. Then unzipped his fly.

She heard the sharp buzz. Her head turned upwards. A shot of excitement blew through her. *She's finally going to get to see 'it'.*

Rock's penis sprang out suddenly, fully erect and free.

"Oh god." Tara instinctively jumped back on her haunches.

Rock winked at her. *Big isn't it?*

She regained her composure – replied only with a slow nod.

"Well what do you think?" Rock's face looked hopeful, but he already knew the answer.

Tara's eyes darted around the room.

Rock gestured with his hand. "Go on. Describe it."

"Wha…?"

"What does it look like?"

"Ah…what do you mean?"

Rock frowned. *She wasn't understanding the game.* He tried something different. "I command you to describe it for me."

Command? She questioned to herself, eyebrows

raised. But she liked a man to take control so she complied.

"Ah…it's…bumpy?"

He frowned. "What do you mean bumpy?"

"I mean, you know…soldier-esk."

She was speechless – obviously taken aback by his big package…*his very big package.*

He let his face drop. "You can't come up with a better description than that?" He meant it to be an order.

Tara took another look. *Fuck it was big.*

He grew impatient. "Come on, describe it." It was an order. "What do you see?"

She knew she would have to obey his commands.

Wanting to please her master, she described in quick succession what she saw. "Thick, blue-ish purple vein, covered by goosebumpy, chicken flesh skin." She looked again. "And a big handful of weather beaten, elephant skin like sagging balls, shrunk down like an accordion."

He raised an eyebrow at her, hands on his hips. *More.*

"Ah…big…massive penis sprouting from a bushy bed of sort of darkish, curly hair?"

Rock noticed a moment of uncertainty flash over Tara's eyes. *She's thinking about what it would be like inside her.*

Then Rock's demeanour turned sly. Now that the introductions were out of the way, and she'd met the big fella, it was time to get down to business. Besides, he was starting to flop around like a cock in a sock.

"Hey, Tara." He placed a finger under her chin as

he searched her eyes, scorching them with his searing intent.

She looked up at him. She melted. *Anything you want Rock.*

"Now that my thermometer is up, why don't you take your temperature.'"

Max Martin chuckled to himself. "Take your temperature." *Good one.* He'd finish writing the sex part later. *Time for lunch.*

His hopes of a career writing mummy porn were looking up. He strolled into the kitchen, delighted with his work. Another phrase sprang to mind – *'she's getting jiggy with Mr Biggie'.*

He grinned like a Cheshire cat – *better write that down.*

Chapter Nine

Eight days after Max first put fingers to the keyboard, he found himself standing in one of his most hated places. *The city!*

Brisbane city to be exact and he was smack bang in the middle of it. As cities go, he supposed this one wasn't so bad. But he was sweating, his stomach grumbled and he glared up at the buildings with confusion etched across his face. He breathed in a deep, calming breath and felt a shot of damp, suffocating heat surge down into his lungs. *Typical Queensland summer.*

Max hovered in the Queen Street Mall – he knew he'd arrived in the mall, because he'd just passed through a giant archway which marked one of its entrances and which stated "Queen Street Mall".

The mall's wide, paved streets were cut off to vehicles – only foot traffic allowed – and the streets were alive with activity. Max stared up at the giant shops, looming above him. Glittering names and glossy displays lured in their prey. But not Max – he was immune to their charms. Max was here on a mission.

Before he'd left home earlier that day, he'd fashioned a list of potential publishers for his manuscript, compliments of the yellow pages. His plan of attack was simple – turn up, walk in and show them the manuscript. He wasn't completely naïve. He figured he'd probably get a couple of rejections – which is why he'd put a few names on his list.

And now if he could just find the first address on the list, he'd be able to get this mission started, over with and then get the hell out of this rat race. He cringed at the swarms rushing past. The mall was a kaleidoscope of people – shoppers, businesspeople, students, backpackers, tourists – all rushing – or being pulled, like magnets to their destinations. Max watched them go – *crazy ants!*

He crumpled the paper in his hand, as he scoured the shop fronts again, trying to pick up the numbers. *Damn numbers, where are they?* Some stores wore their numbers like proud badges, others made them infuriatingly invisible.

He glanced sideways in the nick of time to see a flock of people bearing down on him. He stepped back for fear of being stampeded. Unfortunately, he stepped back into the path of an equivalent flock coming from the other direction. Elbows poked into him, bags scratched him and perfumes and body sprays invaded his nostrils. He got jostled about by both groups, diverging around him like he was a rock embedded in a river.

He ejected from the flurry next to a tall tree, which

was landscaped into a huge, rectangular pot. He flopped down on its edge, which doubled as a seat, and took a breath. He shook his head. *Fuck this.*

He straightened out the paper in his hand and examined his list again. *Maybe he had the number wrong.* He figured on finding the publishers more quickly than this, since it was a Friday morning and he'd expected the mall to be quieter.

He blew out a frustrated breath and scanned the shop fronts again, filtering out anything retail and focusing on any entrance, corridor or flight of stairs that might lead him to the publisher's office. He'd driven more than three hours this morning and he wasn't leaving until someone saw his manuscript.

Damn it! He couldn't find it. *Maybe the wrong side?* He flung his head around, and peered across the wide pathway to the multitude of temptations on the other side of the mall. *Maybe over there.*

He started across the pathway, and as soon as he did, he was hit by the smell of open air cooking. He glanced at his watch – *nearly lunch time.* His stomach growled as if in response to the cocktail of aromas that now penetrated deep into his nostrils.

He inhaled the wafts of culinary delights, tempted to just eat and leave. He spotted buskers setting up nearby. They tested their instruments, scratching the air with their start up routines. He squinted as if he was in pain – *the noise.* He tried to screen out the noise – buskers, people – *too many people.* His head reverberated with the angry buzz of the crowds.

If he didn't want this so much, he would just turn around and head back home. But, desperate to achieve his goal of writing and selling an erotica book, he'd bitten the bullet and made the trip – *he couldn't leave yet.*

His only confidant in this whole thing was his best mate Baldo. He'd told Baldo about his plans for Brisbane.

"Not sure that's how you go about it Max." Baldo had warned with one eyebrow in the air. "Want me to come with you?"

"Thanks, but this is something I gotta do myself."

Max now stood motionless in the city – *maybe should've brought Baldo.* He glanced in the direction of the hotel he'd booked for the night. *Might be able to ask them for directions.* He'd checked into a hotel in the city, so there'd be no need to drive around the streets or worry about parking. *Good tip Baldo.*

It was supposed to make it easier. But he'd found the street names confusing – especially those with different names left and right of the same street. Add to that, the many detours on the sidewalks from construction in the city. If it wasn't for that archway into the mall, he would've been lost – completely.

The now melodic tunes of the buskers reached fever pitch. Max snapped out of his reverie. He turned a full circle, and watched as people crisscrossed from every direction. He was under siege.

His eye caught a line of people disappearing into the pavement – then a little blue sign explained – "bus entrances". *Nothing like that back home.*

He let his eyes drift upwards from the blue sign and then he saw it.

There it is – finally! The number he'd been looking for – the first publisher on his list. "Thank Christ."

He muttered.

He strode over to the thin corridor entrance, found the small bank of elevators, and rode one of them to the fourth floor. The doors thumped open and he stepped out with a hint of uneasiness.

He was instantly swathed in an offensive dank, mustiness which he assumed was coming from the old, brown carpet in the hallway. He twitched his nose pretending not to notice and proceeded down the hallway towards a set of glass doors. He felt the cool rush of the air-conditioner, thankful for the welcome relief.

He glanced out of the sparse windows which gave surprisingly generous views of the city. It was another world – different to his home – there were no buildings this tall back home and…*was there even an elevator?* The strangeness of where he was hit home. He shivered – a twinge of doubt snaked over him – but he shook it away.

He took a peek at his clothes, his brow furrowed. *Was he under dressed?* He checked his t-shirt, shorts and thongs – a flannel shirt draped over his arm. He slung the shirt back on, shoved his arms through the sleeves and neatened it as best he could.

As he approached the glass doors, emblazoned with the publisher's name, a shot of uncertainty rippled through him. He stole a quick breath, tightened his grip on his manuscript in one hand, checked the list in the other, then ploughed through the glass doors.

A set of eyes snapped up at him as he let the doors swing closed behind him.

He was immediately in a small, empty waiting room

— wooden panelled and looked like it hadn't left the seventies. Then he spotted a young woman, almost hidden from view behind a huge, wooden reception counter.

He strolled up, cleared his throat and smiled. "Hi."

"Can I help you?" The receptionist asked, her young, petite looks belied her professional manner.

Max shuffled a foot in his thong. "Ah, yeah, I'm here to see someone about getting my manuscript published."

"Do you have an appointment?" she asked, with a flick of her brown fringe and wearing a confused expression. *That was unexpected.*

She'd thought he was here to make a delivery or something by the look of him. She couldn't stop an eyebrow tugging upwards at the sight of the visitor dressed in a flannel shirt over a black print t-shirt, sports shorts and…*were those thongs?*

Max cleared his throat again. "Well no I don't have an appointment. But I don't need much of Mr…ah…." He checked his list. "Johnson's time."

"Who's your agent sir?" She held her pen over a message pad ready to jot down the details.

He shook his head. "Don't have one."

She glared up at him. "You don't have one?"

"Nope."

"Ok." She fidgeted with the message pad. "Have you published before sir?"

"Nope. First time."

She put the pen down. *Okay.* She eyed the visitor with growing skepticism. "Did Mr Johnson know you were coming?"

"Nope. Never met him." He laid a hopeful hand on the counter.

The receptionist pushed the message pad to one side on the desk. "Okay. Sir, we have a process for unsolicited manuscripts." She pulled out a drawer in the desk and grabbed some forms. "I can give you the details so that you can-"

"Wait." Max cut her off. He leaned into the counter, a sunburnt arm slipped across the top. He glanced at the name tag pinned to her left breast. "Mandy." His smile was sheepish. "Can't I just hand it to Mr Johnson now?" *Fuck was he flirting with this young sprig?*

Mandy giggled a nervous response. "No, that's not really how we operate."

He flashed his sweetest smile. "Can you make an exception?" He groaned on the inside – *letch*.

"Sir." Mandy's voice was soft. She looked him straight in the eyes. *He wasn't half bad for an old guy.* "There's a process that all ah…writers, need to go through." She switched on the spiel. "We at Johnson, Mars & Tate Publishing don't usually accept unsolicited manuscripts." She held up a finger. "Except, we do in October – for one month – to give independent authors an opportunity to submit their work." She beamed out a high wattage smile demonstrating her pride at her employer's generosity.

"October?" Max pulled his arm back from the counter. "But I'm here now. It's December. I can't wait another ten months."

Mandy's smile disintegrated.

"Does it really matter if I give it to you in

December?" His voice shaky and hopeful.

"Sir, it's just that we have a process." It's all she could do to reiterate, aware that she was alone in the office with this man.

"Yeah, I heard ya. A process." He frowned and took a step back. *Didn't want to scare the girl.* "I just want someone to have a look at it and see if it's ok."

Mandy sighed. *You've got to be kidding.* "Look," she said, pen in the air. "I'll tell you what." Then she locked onto his eyes, with a focus intended to convey that his manuscript was the most important thing in the world to her. "My boss will be back from lunch soon. How about you leave your manuscript and details with me and I promise I'll show it to him." She put her pen down on the desk, it was a done deal. "How does that sound?"

Max shrugged. "I guess. If that's the best you can do." He handed over his beloved manuscript.

She saw the document, and her eyebrows shot up. His manuscript was small, thin – tiny really. *Was this guy for real?* His manuscript was a fraction of the usual size that they dealt with. She flashed him a fake smile and placed the manuscript on the desk beside her.

Then she went through the charade of gathering Max's name and contact details. She jotted them down on a sticky note and slapped them on the manuscript, giving the document a pat, and its owner a reassuring smile. Then she turned her eyes down toward her keyboard and started tapping at the keys – back to work.

Max smiled and nodded. *What now?*

He turned around and examined the humble waiting

room. A couple of plain chairs in the corner looked inviting. He noticed a small coffee table with a pile of reading material neatly stacked on top. *That'll do.* He strolled over to a chair and sat down.

He glanced up occasionally at two wooden doors on either side of the reception counter. He presumed they led to offices and expected the publisher himself to exit or enter at least one of them. He wasn't going to miss his chance to see Mr Johnson of Johnson, Mars & Tate Publishing.

Mandy glanced up at the visitor, unable to hide the surprise in her voice. "Sir?"

"I don't mind waiting." Max waved a hand.

"He might be a little while yet."

"No problems."

Mandy looked away. *Crap. It didn't work. He was still here.* She tried a different approach. "Ah…Mr Johnson may not have time to look over your manuscript right away."

"Yeah ok, but I was still hoping to talk to him." His voice firm. "Besides, that's my only copy."

He smiled, pointing to his manuscript. It was true – he only had one good copy – a second copy, back at the hotel, had gotten dirty. "I'll need it back after your boss looks at." *In case I have to take it to another publisher.*

Mandy mentally rolled her eyes. She could make a copy for him and then he'd be on his way. But she'd been warned before about excessive use of the photocopier. Hopefully her boss would be back soon.

She snuck a peek at Max again, and watched as he grabbed a magazine from the small coffee table and made himself comfortable. She caught another glimpse of his footwear and grinned – *probably his best pair of thongs.*

Suddenly Max looked up, caught her staring at him. "Something wrong?"

Crap! "No, I was just…ah…taking a look at your manuscript here." She patted it, picked it up and flipped it open.

Max nodded with enthusiasm. "Good isn't it." He watched her.

She saw him watching. *Crap.* Now she'd have to make a show of reading it. She flipped over the pages and landed more than half way through the stack – it was a small stack. She pitched her eyes on the words, and absently read a few lines to herself. Then she read a few more. Then her eyes were practically glued to the page. *Unbelievable!* She kept reading.

'Tara looked up at Rock, excitement in her eyes, practically panting like a dog. "Yes Rock, I would love to take your temperature. Anything for you." The warmth from the fire making her feel loose and willing to obey.

Tara, still kneeling in front of Rock on the super soft blanket, opened her mouth, looked up at Rock for a second with a twinkle in her eye, licked her lips, then leaned in and wrapped her trout pout around his penis…his very, very big penis.

She gagged as his penis filled up her mouth and she felt it hit deep inside her throat. *Fuck it's a big penis. Rock you really delivered.*

Rock Hard was so excited. He loved it when they saw what a big man he was and what he had to offer them. He rolled his eyes, he could barely contain the buildup he could feel ready to erupt inside him. He reached down and gently grabbed a handful of Tara's hair and pushed her head towards his groin.

She moaned out in response, reached above her head with her free hand, took hold of his and moved it down by his side.

God she made him feel so good. "That's it baby. You're doing a fucking great job.'"

Mandy's eyebrows shot half way up her forehead. *Jesus!*

She glanced up at Max in the waiting room.

He was already watching her, with heavy expectation.

She hesitated. "So, you say that this is meant to be erotica?" She forced her eyebrows back down, but left them furrowed. "I mean proper erotica…for women? You weren't trying to do a send up or…spoof…or…anything?" *Aside from the editing – or lack of it.*

Max was up on his feet, excitement coursed through his veins at the hint of genuine interest. "Nah, nah, it's real erotica."

"Ok." Her voice even, her eyes darted away from his. *Wait until the boss sees this.* She smiled to herself.

Max took the cue and sat back down. *Let her read some more. This is going well.*

Not more than thirty minutes later, the glass doors suddenly burst open and a very tall and busy man breezed in. He immediately barked orders at his receptionist.

"Mandy, can you arrange for this to be delivered to Sophie please." He handed her a thick wad wrapped in brown paper.

"Yes Mr Johnson." Mandy plonked down Max's manuscript and took the brown wad – she was all business.

Mr Johnson? Max stood as he heard the name.

Johnson caught the movement in his peripheral vision. He had been planning to disappear through one of the doors into his office. But now he turned and looked at the man in the waiting room – noting his less than business attire.

Johnson didn't bother to introduce himself. He simply glared over at Mandy with an expectant look.

"Sir, Mr…?" She glanced at the sticky note on the manuscript. "Martin…Max Martin, is here to see you about getting his manuscript published."

She held up the paltry offering.

Johnson squinted. "Unsolicited?"

His receptionist gave him a few short, sharp nods.

"Mr Martin." Johnson turned back to the visitor in the waiting room.

"Max."

"Max." Johnson took a quick breath. "I'm sure Mandy here has explained the process for submitting unsolicited manuscripts."

Max looked at him confused. *There's those words again.* "Well yes-"

"Mandy." Johnson said her name like it was an order. "Will give you the details of when and where to submit your work." In one quick motion, he turned and started through one of the wooden doors.

Max could only watch him go.

But Mandy took action. She made a real show of it. She got up from her seat, manuscript in hand and started to follow her boss. "Ah sir, if you could just…."

She raised her index finger in Max's direction. "Just give me a minute." And then she disappeared through the door behind her boss.

Safely behind the door Mandy engaged in loud, urgent whispering with her boss, suggestive of more than just a professional relationship.

"Did you try and get rid of him Mandy?"

"Of course I did, of course I did. I was here on my own. I didn't feel comfortable making a scene with him."

Johnson nodded. "Of course, sorry."

She rolled her eyes at him. "Anyway I told him you'd look at his stuff."

"What?" His whisper a bit too loud. "Come on Mandy, you know better than that."

"I know," she said, then broke out into a huge grin.

She held up the manuscript. "But it's so bad, I thought you could get a good laugh out of it." She snickered mischievously, then poked him in the chest. "Then you can tell him it's no good."

He huffed. "Oh, ok." Anything to get rid of the guy – he had real clients to deal with.

Mandy flipped open the pages and shoved it towards her boss.

Johnson ran his eyes over the page, skimming it with a practiced speed. Then his eyes bulged as he read.

'Rock rocked his pelvis as Tara serviced his member. He knew he wasn't going to be able to hold on for long. But he wanted her to enjoy it too. He pushed his penis into Tara's mouth as far as he could manage. He enjoyed the soft feel of her warm lips wrapped around him.

Tara gagged again. She gripped onto Rock's hips, riding the waves while his penis moved in and out of her mouth. She gagged each time it hit the back of her throat.

It excited him so much, he could feel the quivering of his eruption coming. And then he exploded. "Oh, god. Baby. Oh…ah…." He grunted. It felt so good, and it seemed to take an eternity to subside.

But when it did, he looked down at Tara, the remains of his pleasure streaked across her cheeks. He smiled his satisfied best as he looked down into her eyes. "Was that good for you too baby?"'

Johnson snorted as he flipped closed the manuscript. "God it is bad! And he uses the 'P' word."

Mandy chuckled. She checked her noise level — didn't want the guy in the waiting room to hear.

"Did he say it was a joke or satire?"

She shook her head. "No, he intends it to be erotica for women."

Johnson scoffed. "Well it's obviously not that — at least not for women's pleasure." *Erotica for men maybe.* "Ok, I'll talk to him."

They opened the door, and entered the waiting room like naughty school children.

Mandy composed herself and returned to her desk. She glanced up at Max. "Mr Johnson wants a word with you."

Max's heart leapt. *Wow, it's gonna happen.* He stood up, pulled down the edges of his flannel shirt and waited for Johnson to speak.

Johnson extended a hand. "Mr Martin." He said it as if he was announcing it.

Max shook his hand.

They didn't sit.

"Look, I…appreciate the effort you've gone to here."

Max smiled. *It certainly was that – eight days of solid writing.*

He cut to the chase. "Thank you for bringing this in."

Max smiled. *No worries.*

Then the publisher dropped an anvil on his head. "I'm sorry. It's not for us." Just like that.

What? Max's eyes were wide. "What do you mean?"

Johnson fidgeted with his tie. "Look, I'm sure you've put your…heart and soul into this-" He cut himself off as he flashed a look at Mandy.

She was watching – and listening.

He flicked back to Max. "But, it's not quite the sort of thing that we're looking for."

Max rubbed his goatee. "I don't understand. You publish erotica books for women. This is an erotica book." He looked at his stack of papers, and suddenly saw the measly offering for what it was – small. "Well, I can add to it if that's what it needs…for a fee. You guys pay in advance don't you?"

Johnson couldn't contain the laughter that came spewing forth. He let it rip out of him along with his arrogance. "Am I being punked or something?" He stepped back and looked around.

Max was confused. "No mate. It's no joke."

Johnson let the laugh subside gradually, until it trickled to a stop. "I'm sorry. Look mate. I was trying to let you down gently, but honestly…." He pointed to the papers in his hand. "This isn't any good, not as erotica for women – not the kind that we publish."

But a sudden pang of compassion compelled him to add. "Look, someone might pick it up…with a bit of work…and editing." And then he added some useful advice for good measure. "I'll tell you what. Work on it, improve it, get it edited, and send it back in October – through the proper channels."

October? Max felt his heart sink. It was as if the floor had opened up and his insides were being ripped out and hurled into the void. As hard a man as he was, he couldn't keep the disappointment off his face. He hadn't steeled himself for how this complete rejection would feel. He thought he might get some feedback, but honestly believed he'd produced a pretty good product.

Johnson put a hand on his shoulder to lead him out the door.

Max didn't resist.

"Look buddy. If it makes you feel any better, you're not the first wannabe writer to walk in here wearing their heart on their sleeve." He sighed before further enlightening Max with his wisdom. "Sometimes we truly let ourselves believe something is really good…until someone tells us that it isn't. Don't beat yourself up over it."

Max cocked an eye at him. *No, that doesn't really help.* His head thumped with embarrassment, disappointment and hunger. He let Johnson lead him out, without a fight, through the glass doors, and forgetting his manuscript.

He let the doors close behind him, and stood in the hallway, transfixed. *Did he hear that right?* Johnson's words regurgitated in his head. *"Not erotica. Not good." How could that be? He worked so hard.*

Mandy watched Max Martin amble back down the hallway. A moment of guilt flushed over her. His look of devastation was so complete. It was only then that she wondered about him – as a person. *What could his life be like, that could cause him to look so beaten after one rejection?* "Sorry Max." She whispered.

But nobody heard.

***

Max wandered aimlessly for an hour or so around Brisbane's city streets. He no longer heard the angry buzz of the crowds or the buskers playing. He no longer noticed how much he got jostled. His thoughts were consumed by his own monumental failure – his own personal black rain cloud hovered over him, lingering still – even after it'd dumped its cold, wet load on him.

He should have tried the next publisher on his list. He should have shrugged off Johnson and his gut-wrenching assessment of his work. And he shouldn't have let it get to him. But it did get to him. And worse, it changed something inside him.

For the first time since he'd started this project, he had doubts – big doubts. *What if he really wasn't any good?* He kicked a non-existent stone on the footpath. His brain spun at the sudden realisation that his work might be no good and that he might be wasting his time.

He felt the burden of the events of the past weeks press heavy on his heart – screwing things up with Jenna, losing his job, the display at the local pub, trying to pay his mortgage.

But worse than that, he felt his confidence shatter – splintered by dejection, his nerve now raw and exposed. If he didn't get a grip, he'd lose that too.

He sighed. *Now what?* Reality's bite felt vicious and cold.

And his stomach was still growling. He eyed a small café across the road and considered its all you can eat lunchtime offering. But what really caught his eye and which was more apt for how he was feeling, was the glittery, shiny pub next door. *That's better.*

The pub looked a bit flashier than his usual hangouts back home, but hey – *a pub's a pub.* He tapped out a message on his phone for Baldo. *'Manuscript sucks, life sucks, going to get drunk.'*

He knew Baldo would seek him out later for more details. But in the meantime, he needed to boost his spirits – lots of them.

He straightened his shoulders, scooted across the busy road, grabbed onto one of the big, silver door handles, swung open the heavy, wooden door and marched up to the bar.

Chapter Ten

Katherine stepped out along the uneven, bricked pavement, as if she was stepping on submerged rocks in a river, carefully pre-selecting a path over the ground to ensure safe passage in her evening heels. This was a notorious street for heels – and she had no desire to trip or overbalance – and she definitely did not want to suffer the humiliation of a complete and undignified collapse on the pavement.

Her date flicked her a curious look. "You right there?"

"Uh huh." She nodded, her eyes landing on Steven's comfortable shoes. She frowned and tried to fall into sync with his stride.

They dodged the throngs of people that swept past them, some squeezing themselves through non-existent gaps.

Steven groaned and shook his head. People couldn't be bothered travelling in a consistent direction on the footpath.

They finally reached a stretch of flat surface.

Katherine smiled with relief. *Thank god.* She felt her shoulders drop back down as she settled into a more natural step. "That's better."

She glanced sideways at her companion. Steven did look rather handsome tonight in his grey suit and blue tie. *Perfect for a dinner date.*

She waited for him to notice her.

Nothing. Not even a glance. He seemed absorbed.

In fact, there'd hardly been any talking between them at all in the last twenty minutes. Katherine had quick-changed into her evening dress at work, and met Steven at six o'clock on the dot, as requested, in the foyer of their building.

He'd greeted her with a light kiss on the cheek, complimented her on her dress – it was a very sexy dress – and that was it. Since then, they'd strolled along in an awkward silence. *Or maybe it was her guilty conscience.*

In any case, conversation had shrivelled up like dust and blown away in the wind. Except that – there was no wind tonight. It was a beautiful, still night.

Katherine inhaled the warm night air and admired the glitzy shops and aromatic venues all vying for their attention. The sights, the smells, the sounds – she felt her heart beat a little faster. *How she loved the city.* It was animated, loud and – *alive!* All the things she wasn't inside. She shivered as a tingle buzzed through her.

Steven offered her his jacket.

"No thanks." She smiled, grateful that he at least seemed aware of her presence.

She rubbed a hand over her bare shoulder and flicked her eyes out into the distance – the horizon still visible. It didn't fail her. *Dusk on an early summer evening.* The city was in a holding pattern – hovering between day and night – awaiting its transformation from business to play, when the darkness illuminated the city, switching on its sparkle.

Katherine loved that part the most. She loved many things about the city – its bustle, its vibrant activity, particularly at the end of the work week, its cultures, but mostly – she loved its sparkle.

As the sun dipped down, remnants of daylight lingered – and it was that gap, before day completely surrendered to night – that held the promise. An unfilled expectation that the night could be anything – that the city could deliver your every desire.

She let out a quick breath and smiled out at the city. Her serenity interrupted only by a niggling voice in the far recesses of her mind – her mother's words. *"Chasing the bright lights of the city Katherine."* She could never understand why that should be a bad thing. She shook the voice away.

Her mind spun with more important matters tonight. She had a decision to make. And she'd better make it soon because she and Steven had almost arrived at the destination for their dinner date.

They turned into Edward Street, a busy and popular inner street in the centre of the city. *Not far now.*

Katherine's doubts about her relationship with Steven had ballooned. Now they were big doubts. Break up kind of doubts. She'd ventured into unchartered waters – *for her anyway* – because for the first time in her adult life, she questioned her choice of men.

Damn Sally. Her housemate and friend was the catalyst for her deviation from the status quo – and as much as she wanted it to be just a glitch, it pained her to admit that her friend might be right.

She stole a quick glance at Steven. Sure he ticked all her boxes – *but was she ticking off the wrong boxes?* He was still attractive, she still liked his thick, dark hair, he was still nice and tall, she loved his bright blue eyes, he was well dressed, impeccably groomed – tick, tick, tick – *what was not to like?*

Add to all that, he had a solid job – an accountant – he'd rarely be out of work. He liked the city, and they had a lot in common. He could be romantic. All good ticks.

She mentally slapped herself. There was no reason not to like him. *What was she thinking breaking up with him?* He's not that bad. *Honestly, what's missing?* She asked herself again, louder, and she actually thought she'd spoken the question out loud.

"You're quiet tonight Katherine."

She snapped out of her reverie. *It wasn't quiet inside her head.* Her face flashed surprise, thoughts interrupted. "Just thinking." She covered. *Original.*

He peered at her, then cut his eyes back to the front. "Anything you care to share with me?" His voice, smooth and measured.

She gave him a little shake of her head in response, but she felt sure he could see straight through her.

They passed a shop window – stylish, classy, silky smooth exterior. Katherine caught a glimpse of Steven and herself in the glass wall. It reflected back what looked like a well suited couple. *So what was her problem?*

She sighed. She wanted the answer – desperately. Then she wouldn't be about to break off her relationship with Steven based solely on some flimsy feeling that something was – *missing.*

She couldn't put it off much longer. She owed it to herself – and to Steven for that matter – to do the right thing. *Where to start?*

Steven's gaze softened. "You look really beautiful tonight."

She certainly did. She'd picked out her emerald green, calf-length, dress that gently hugged her in all the right places and billowed out lightly behind her as she moved. She loved how soft and sexy the fabric felt against her skin – and the smattering of shimmer on the shoulder straps added a touch of class.

Her date smiled at her, warmth creeping back into his lips. "Green brings out the colour of your eyes."

She offered him a thin smile in return. "Thanks." Then flicked her eyes away. A pang of guilt stung her gut.

They walked passed a lunchtime café that was now closed. But the city pub next door looked like it might start hopping soon.

Katherine raised a hopeful eyebrow at Steven.

"No. I don't think so. We already have reservations elsewhere."

She shrugged. "Was worth a shot."

Steven never took her to a pub. *"Bit low brow,"* he'd say. But this pub didn't look low brow to her. On the contrary, it was considerably upmarket. At least, that's what its name implied – or rather, stated. Shiny, gold lettering running across the glass and wood door, stamped it clearly as, "The Upmarket Bar".

Katherine spotted an arty, metal bench seat on the street at the front of the pub. Her eyes grew wide with delight. *How quaint.*

And her voice turned strangely urgent. "Let's sit."

Steven knitted his brows together. "Here?" He glanced around. "Really?"

She nodded. *Yes.*

He turned his nose up as he glared down at the seat. Then shrugged. "Ok, if that's what you want."

She sat down first and rested her little, black bag in her lap, then watched as her date appeared to perform a strange ritual.

He took off his jacket, stepped slowly over to the seat, turned around and perched on the end of it, his jacket resting in his lap.

She watched him. *Germ phobia?* Then she studied him more closely. *What was she looking for?* She shuffled a shoe forward and back – overwhelmed by the feeling that she should be looking for something. *A sign? But a sign of what? To tell her whether to dump him or not?*

He turned his head towards her, careful not to move too much in the seat. "So, did you want to tell me what's on your mind?"

She opened her mouth to speak, but a sudden noise rang out from inside the bar. Like a door opening and the noise rushing out for a few seconds – then it was gone. She glanced up and tried to peer inside. The pub's glitzy glass exterior gave nothing away. *One way tint?*

Steven pointed to the door. "Did you want to go in there?"

She flicked him an expectant look. *Maybe there was some hope after all.* "Do you?"

"No." His voice was flat.

She sunk with disappointment. And then it happened. That was the moment, right there. The uncertainty that had lurked in the wings of her mind, now threaded itself around a rope and grapple, swung out wildly and hooked onto her consciousness. And suddenly she just knew. *It's not going to work out with Steven.*

Her mind raced, her thoughts tripping over themselves. In an instant, her hopes of a family in the future evaporated. If Steven wasn't the man for her, *then who was? What man could be?* If someone as good as Steven didn't do it for her, *what hope did she have?*

A moment of panic stung her. She's thirty-two. What if Steven was her last chance? If she throws this away will she find anyone else? *But who else?* How could she explain this to Steven if she didn't understand it herself? So many questions – and not one, damn, single answer.

"Katherine, please tell what you're thinking about?" His voice came out of nowhere.

She jumped. "Oh. Nothing really." She blew out a quick breath and examined her feet. She'd made the decision – *hadn't she?* Yes. Sure the guilt she felt over telling him was sickening, but the bigger blow was the realisation that Steven just wasn't the one.

"Steven." She glanced away, then back to him. "What do you want in a woman?"

His mouth turned up at the corners, but it wasn't quite a smile. He looked pained, like he had to really think hard. "Where is this coming from Katherine?"

She shook her head – *nowhere*. She drew in a heavy breath and then fixed a suspicious gaze on him – almost accusatory.

Then she blurted out something strange and unexpected – even to her. "Why do you always call me 'Katherine'?"

He looked at her like she'd gone bonkers. "Because that's your name?"

Right. "Uh..huh." Eyes back to the pavement, guilt mounting, gut twisting. This was harder than she thought.

"Well what did you expect me to say Katherine?"

I don't know. Probably just that.

"Do you want me to call you something else?" He frowned. He was lost.

She gave him a strained glance then wrenched her eyes away from him. "No, I…." She smiled. "It doesn't matter." *Shouldn't have said anything.*

He shrugged. "Ok."

Is that it?

She pursed her lips as if she was going to whistle. "It's just that." She locked onto his eyes again, watching for his reaction. "Sal calls me 'Kat'."

"Look…Katherine." His voice suddenly stern. "From what you've told me about your housemate-"

"And friend." Katherine added. *Not the reaction she'd hoped for.*

"Ok." He rolled his eyes. "From what you've told me about your friend, I'm not sure she's the best kind of person for you to be spending a lot of time with."

What? "We live together."

"I know that." His tone coated with condescension. "It's just, she sounds very flighty." He tapped a finger to his temple to demonstrate. "You know, not much upstairs. "I know the type – she'll fill your head with all sorts of rot."

Wow. She was gob smacked.

"She manages a coffee shop." Katherine reminded him. "She can't be too, you know." She imitated his action with a finger to her own temple. "Missing upstairs."

He straightened his neatly laid jacket. His voice softer. "I've offended you. I'm sorry."

He earned himself a brief reprieve – but the damage was already done. *He's a snob. How did I not see this before?*

Steven stood up and slung his jacket over his shoulder. He reached out for her hand. She let him pull her to her feet.

"I'm sorry Katherine. I didn't mean to sound harsh." He leaned down just enough to zero in on her eyes. "I know you live with her now. It's just that down the track, when you have your own place, or we move in together."

Wow! That thought was suddenly a little distressing. She cringed on the inside. *Something didn't feel right.*

"Did you hear me?" he was saying.

She nodded, speechless.

"I was saying that in the future, I don't think you should see her anymore."

Katherine suddenly felt like her feet were made of lead. A surge of distress cut a path along her skin. *Breathe.*

She stood tall. "You know – that's funny. Because that's what she said about you." *Did she just say that to Steven?*

She felt like she'd just turned a corner in their relationship – and straight down towards a dead end.

She looked at him – really looked at him. She saw a different person. *Had he changed? Or had she?* She honestly couldn't tell.

"Steven." Her voice calm, but laced with determination as she delivered her verdict. "I'm not sure it's going to work out between us."

***

Katherine lowered the cool glass of lemonade onto a coaster, her fingers sliding through the condensation forming on the outside of the glass. She'd picked a quiet, out of the way booth and nestled in. Sally was on her way.

"Won't be long." Sally promised over the phone. "About an hour," she'd said. Had to get ready, but she was definitely coming.

As soon as Katherine filled her in on the situation with Steven, she was on her way – at least she'd planned to be. She was coming for the debrief – the relationship break up debrief. And for support of course.

But also because Katherine was staying in the city for a while – in a bar! Sally jumped at the opportunity – her makeshift plan of attack was, "I'll meet you in the city. We can make a night of it."

Not that Katherine was big on 'making a night' of anything, but with no contingency plan after she'd dumped Steven – and she was still wearing that killer dress – she'd decided to stay in her beloved city for the evening, and see what surprises it held.

Sally's words still rang in her ears. *"You ditched him! I can't believe you did it!"* Followed by, *"You're going to a bar?"*

Fair enough. Katherine Wilkins did not typically frequent bars, but it was where she was left standing after Steven abruptly departed.

"I'm sorry you feel that way Katherine," he'd said to her. To be fair, he didn't totally run. He did first offer to walk her to her car, but she'd declined.

Did she just make a big mistake?

She'd found herself standing alone outside of The Upmarket Bar. It felt like a certain serendipity to just walk right in, order a drink and sit down.

"It's not just an old pub." Katherine had giggled to Sal on the phone. "It's actually quite nice – classy even." Then out of nowhere, something possessed her to say, "Maybe I'll meet Mr Right."

Sally hooted into the phone loud and clear. "In a bar?" Then the warning. "Honey, you won't meet anyone nice in a bar."

To which Katherine had retorted. "I thought you said I shouldn't date anyone 'nice'."

The silence on Sally's end of the phone was deafening. *Touché.*

Then Sally had fired off a parting shot. "Just don't do anything crazy until I get there. Promise me."

Crazy. Ha! She'd never done anything crazy in her life.

"Text me when you're close." She'd told Sally.

That was half an hour ago.

Katherine wiggled till she was comfortable on the soft, cream leather seat. The high back booths on her left and right made conditions perfect for what she had in mind.

Her eyes darted around the room – quick check – *not many here yet – just a drunk at the bar crying in his beer.* She'd noticed him when she'd slipped up to order her lemonade. She'd picked a moment when the man was distracted, then grabbed her drink and slipped back to the booth. She'd practiced the art of invisibility her whole life. *A woman's first line of defence.*

She took one more glance around the modern, two-toned black and grey sleek décor. *Coast is clear.* Then she reached into her handbag, and slid out her little rectangular piece of heaven – her reading tablet. She'd finally bought one and loaded her favourite books onto it.

She felt her heart beat a little faster as she switched on the tablet. She was seconds away from once again secretly devouring the pages of her 'naughty' book.

Chapter Eleven

Max sat hunched over his half empty pot of beer, arms folded on the bar in front of him. He stared with growing intensity at the glass of beer as if it was about to reveal the secret of life to him – *or at least of women.*

He huffed. Then grunted. Then signalled the bartender. "Another one please!"

The bartender glanced in his direction. *Easy to spot who barked out that order.* The man stuck out like a sore thumb – rough, noisy and under dressed. Besides, the guy had been stewing here since early afternoon. He had hoped he'd be gone before the evening rush arrived.

The man was obviously drowning his sorrows – it was usually only one of two things – women or work. With this guy, he figured it was probably both. He frowned. He supposed he could accommodate him a little longer, but when the punters started to trickle in, the last thing he needed was an angry drunk on his hands – after all, *this was an upmarket city bar.*

The bartender raised an eyebrow at Max. "I think

you might've had enough buddy."

"I'll say when I've had enough." Max lifted his glass and banged it back down. He was making a stand dammit! *Sick of people telling him what to do.* Besides, *Baldo wasn't here yet.*

Max had told him not to come, but he'd insisted – especially after he'd heard about Max's less than successful visit to the publisher earlier that day.

No real surprise there. Max had been on a bender ever since – *and definitely no surprise there.*

"It's only a three hour drive." Baldo reminded him. "It's Friday afternoon – bike shop's closed. I can get someone to cover the short shift on Saturday morning. No problem. I'll be there. Just tell me where you are." Baldo knew his way around the city, but he knew Max would be a fish out of water. *God knows what trouble he'd get himself into when he started drinking.*

The bartender flashed Max a rehearsed smile. He'd come up against this type before – many times. He swiped a cloth along the bar close to Max. "Rough day?" His tone flat but tinged with practiced sincerity.

Max squinted at him. Then resumed his staring contest with his beer. "Yeah, you could say that."

"Women troubles?"

A unexpected bolt of anger blew through him. "Fuckin' women hey!" He shook his head. Grunted. "Not really. But it started out that way."

Then it struck him again. He thumped a hand on the bar. "Got fired – because of a woman." He gave a quick shake of his head. "Now I'm out of work. Out of options. Out of luck." Hearing it out loud – *fuck he felt like a loser.*

The bartender doled out an obligatory response. "Sucks buddy." He pulled the lever on the beer tap to pour another pot for Max, and then set it down in front of him. He smiled. "It's on me." *Guy's a loser — least he could do.*

Max glanced at him, eyes wide. "Thanks mate."

The bartender shrugged. "Wanna talk about it?"

"Don't you have stuff to do?"

"Not right now. Will do soon when the numbers pick up." He lifted a tray of clean glasses out of the dishwasher, and sat it on the bar. "You said earlier you were waiting for a friend. When's he getting here?"

Max rubbed his face with his hand. He wasn't that wasted yet. He released a heavy sigh, the fight draining from him. "Don't worry mate, I won't be any trouble."

Then he dwelled on the words Johnson the publisher had used earlier that day — *to shoot him down.* He mulled them over. *"Not erotica for women."*

Woman's pleasure my arse! He was so sure his plan would work — convinced of it. *How had he gotten it so wrong?* He knew about women — *didn't he?* A hollow feeling rose up in his gut. He was numb — *or at least he would be soon. What was he going to do now? Fuck, what a mess!*

His mate's words rang out in his head. *"Behave yourself Max."* Baldo had warned him. *"I'll be there as soon as I can."* And that was almost an hour ago.

The bartender fussed with some persistent spots on the glasses. He lifted the tray of glasses and placed them in the fridge to chill. The glasses knocked together with a grinding clunk.

Max snapped to attention. Noticed the glasses —

raised an eyebrow at how clean they looked. *Baldo was right – this was an upmarket establishment.*

He glanced down at his clothes. He realised he was still wearing his day wear – flannel shirt over t-shirt on top of shorts, topped off with his best pair of thongs. *How the hell did they let him in here? Must have been a slow afternoon.*

He pointed an index finger in the air, intended for the bartender. His eyes narrowed. "Do you know much about women?"

The bartender dragged the cloth back over the bar where the tray of glasses had stood. He rolled his eyes. "Mate who does?"

Max grunted his agreement.

"Million dollar question isn't it?" The bartender shook his head and put the cloth under the counter.

"Apparently." He scoffed.

"Buddy, I get a lot of women coming in here." He pointed around the room. "Most of the time, I don't think they know what they want."

Amen – ain't that the truth?

"Listen buddy, I gotta set up some tables over here."

Max nodded.

"You're right to stay a bit." He smiled. "Before the night crowd gets here." *And the dress code kicks in.*

Max swivelled on his stool. He only just noticed how really different this place was from his beloved RSL back home. It was quieter for one. The music was soft, not rowdy. The décor was modern in black and grey tones weaved with glass partitions giving a stunningly glitzy effect. *Not bad.*

He saw a small number of businesspeople blending into the background. Suddenly he knew what the bartender was seeing – he was out of place here – *he didn't belong.*

He sighed, and let his eyes wander. *Much like Rock Hard had* – he mused to himself. Then he spotted...*hello pretty lady!*

A woman, no, a vision in green, sat elegantly in the corner booth. *Wow! Now she was dressed right.* He couldn't take his eyes off her. Her beautiful dark hair cascaded over her bare shoulders. She was stunning – *absolutely gorgeous.*

Something stirred inside him. He tapped his fingers with the slightest touch on the bar – *thinking* – his eyes glued to the woman. All thoughts of the mess he was in, vanquished.

He considered his options. He could tell she was in a whole other league than the usual women he tried to pick up. *This might call for a different approach.*

The woman's eyes were glued to something too – but it wasn't him, or anyone else for that matter. Something was drawing her focus downward – *to her lap?*

Max frowned. *What is she doing?* He stared intensely at her – his interest piqued. *What is she...?*

Then he saw it! A swipe of the finger – across a thin, black, rectangle.

A reading tablet! Just like the one the women at the pub back home were reading that night – *that night! The night he made an arse of himself.*

An instant rush of anger and embarrassment flashed back to him. A tsunami of thoughts collided, rushing, forcing their way back in — the women reading the book in the pub, his pathetic manuscript, Johnson's crushing words, Jenna, Mrs Cameron, getting fired by his old mate Frankie — *rejection, rejection, rejection!* His mind was a whirlpool, spinning, sucking him under as he gasped for breath.

A hand touched his shoulder. He jumped up in his seat.

"You ok buddy?" the bartender asked.

Max came out of his trance with a thud. He breathed out quick and loud. "Yeah mate."

The bartender's voice was kinder. "Listen, you want something to eat?" *Poor bastard.*

Max looked up at him, silent resignation dulled his senses. He sighed. "You got any potato chips? Deep fried ones I mean?"

"I can check with our restaurant."

Max nodded. "That would be good, thanks."

He checked his phone while he waited for the bartender to return. Missed call from Baldo — *damn.* And a text — *'Held up in traffic. Be a bit late. Sorry.'*

He sighed.

Then looked over at the woman again — *what was she reading that was so fucking interesting anyway?*

He turned back around to a plate of potato chips in front of him. "That was quick."

"Secret stash." The bartender grinned.

Max turned his attention to the plate of food. He tossed a handful of chips in his mouth as he watched a couple of people come in and out of the bar. He glanced over at the woman periodically. She was still completely engrossed in her book. *I wonder what she's reading?*

Katherine glanced up to see the unkempt drunkard at the bar…watching her. *Oh crap. Caught!* He saw her look up.

She flashed her eyes back down to her reading tablet.

That's right Princess, ignore me. Max watched her with a fierce stare, as if everything that had happened to him recently was her fault.

She peered up again. *What is he looking at? Why is he staring at me?* She took in his physical appearance in a series of quick peeks. *Bogan. Facial hair – disgusting. Poorly dressed.* He might be the hardest, roughest looking man she'd ever seen – but then she worked with businessmen in suits. Without realising it, her eyes had formed a squint and her mouth a matching scowl.

Max cocked an eyebrow. *Is she…smiling at me?* Hard to tell from this distance. *A smile?* Well that changes everything. With the faintest hint and hope of an interested women, Max felt his anger start to slip – then it was a slide – then it avalanched. Then the stirring in his groan started giving the orders.

With the scent of woman on the horizon, he felt his mood lift and he snapped out of his one man pity party in the time it took his heart to beat…once.

Suddenly, he was a man on a mission – a man with hope – and there was a woman to snare.

The bartender noticed the change in the man at the bar. Then he chuckled to himself as he followed the man's gaze towards the women in the green dress in the booth. *Good luck with that buddy. Not a snowflake's chance.*

Max waited until the woman looked up again. She did – only for a half second, but it was all the encouragement he needed. He pasted a smile on his face, lifted his beer in her direction – *cheers* – and winked.

Double crap! Katherine ignored the wink from the weird scruff ball at the bar. Her eyes shifted back to her book – but it was a fruitless task. Contact had been made.

Before she had a chance to react, a figure loomed suddenly in front of her, blocking her line of sight to the bar. *Small relief.*

Max saw the businessman join the lady in green and turned back to the bar and his beer. *Typical, her other half.*

"Hi there." A man in a grey suit and snappy tie beamed down at her, glass of rum and coke in his hand.

She stared wide eyed at her unexpected visitor. "Oh. Um…hi." For a split second, she had visions of Steven coming back for her.

The man ran his free hand through the thick mop of dark overgrowth sprouting from his head. "May I sit down?" He lost his footing for a second, stumbled, caught himself from landing on the table, then righted himself again.

"Oh." Katherine's eyes darted left and right. *He's drunk.*

Mophead held a hand out and gestured again – his face tight. "May I sit down?"

She looked up at him, searching for an excuse. "I'm…ah…waiting for my friend."

He drew his lips back into a thin line. "Right."

"No really." She insisted, glancing in the direction of the front door. "She'll be here any minute?"

His eyebrows shot up. "She?" He mocked. "Like that is it?"

"No." She snapped. "It's not. We're just…." Then she sat bolt upright in her seat. "You know what?" Her tone as firm as she would dare. "I don't have to answer to you." She let her haughty look respond to his initial question. "Please leave me alone."

He took a swig of his drink. "That's a bit mean isn't it bitch?" He leaned in towards her, his eyes glazed. His breath reeking. "I come over here to make nice, and that's how you talk to me."

Katherine started to gather up her things to leave. She leaned around the man to try and catch the bartender's attention.

The man pushed her shoulder and she fell back into the seat. Panic started to build inside her. But she refused to let him see it. She slid back along the booth in an effort to get out from the other side. But he anticipated her move and quickly stepped over to block her path.

Her distress mounted. "Let me out!"

Max heard a woman's high pitched voice – *someone's in trouble*. He spun around in his stool. *The woman at the booth.* He noticed the man leering over her and seemed to be stopping her from getting out of the seat.

Max heard the man say, "Come on love. Just a little introduction." Then he saw him sway.

Maybe not her other half after all.

He started over to the scene. But he barely made it a few steps when he saw the man stumble backwards towards him. *What the…?*

Max laughed when the man turned and he saw the guy's face dripping wet – and the woman holding out her empty glass.

Mophead swiped the drink off his face with his hands. His mouth twitched with anger, his eyes wide. "What the fuck did you do that for you stupid bitch? Look what you've done to my suit!"

The commotion attracted onlookers.

But the man continued, indignant. "I only wanted to talk to you."

Katherine pointed towards the door. Her voice strong and composed. "Newsflash buddy." Her anger spurred her on. "That's not how you talk to a lady. Now leave me alone."

He narrowed his eyes. And thought about hitting back. Instead he settled for, "It's your fucking loss then." Then he slammed his own glass onto the table, splashing his drink. Then he picked up what was left of his dignity and hightailed it to the door.

Max hovered in the wings keeping a watchful eye as the lady in green sat back down in her seat. He grinned – *impressive.*

The bartender suddenly appeared near Max. "Hey buddy."

Startled, Max turned. "Look it wasn't me...no trouble-"

"I know." The bartender smirked and handed him the plate of potato chips. "You left these on the bar."

"Oh." Max took the plate. "Thanks."

The bartender scooted over to Katherine's table, cloth in hand to wipe up the mess.

"Sorry about that." She told him. Then as she watched him skilfully wipe down the table and seat, she was struck by his tall frame, solid build, light brown hair and smooth, boyish face.

"Don't worry about it," he said, oblivious to her interest. He finished the task and headed back to the bar – customers were waiting.

She watched him go – her eyes on a reconnaissance mission, gathering important intel as he resumed his post – *confident stride, nice bod, cute butt.*

He stopped, turned sharply. "Just let me know if you need anything." He offered as an afterthought, completely ignoring the beet red blush that burst across Katherine's face.

Max waited until the bartender was completely finished and tucked safely back behind the bar. Then he took a couple of uneasy steps towards the woman in the green dress. Then stopped in his tracks.

He realised she didn't have a refill yet. *Good idea.* He peddled back to the bar. "Lemonade please." He ordered. It was a guess.

The all-seeing bartender raised an eyebrow at him. *You gotta be kidding buddy.* He knew what Max was up to. *This ought to be good.* He handed Max a tall glass of lemonade – slipped a pink, paper umbrella decoration in it for good measure and smiled a big cheesy grin.

Max frowned. "Thanks."

He turned to head back to the table and the woman in green, when he noticed…*damn, you gotta be kidding!* He saw two young women – both dressed in matching short, sheath dresses and rectangle bags dangling from spaghetti thin shoulder straps. The only visual difference between them seemed to be that one was skinnier than the other. They were standing near the woman in green. *Typical – they run in packs.*

Almost abandoning his quest for a second time, Max froze when he heard one of the women calling the woman in green, a bitch. *Wow this chick's trouble.*

He edged closer so he could hear. He listened intently. It was like a ping pong match.

Skinny Girl said, "We saw you with my boyfriend."

The woman in green replied, "I don't know what you're talking about."

Other Girl said, "Are you having an affair with my friend's boyfriend?"

The woman in green said, "Who are you talking about?"

Skinny Girl said, "The guy you threw a drink on."

"That jerk's your boyfriend?"

Skinny Girl launched herself towards Katherine, claws bared, and took a swipe – but completely missed. "Don't call my boyfriend a jerk!" She screeched.

Katherine once again started out of the booth.

"Ok ladies!" A deep, gravel voice boomed at them.

They jumped, as if a gong had sounded.

They suddenly stopped moving, momentarily shocked.

Skinny Girl's eyes were saucers.

Max planted himself beside the young women in sheaths, his plate of chips in one hand and a pretty looking lemonade in the other.

"Time to break it up ladies."

Katherine sank back into her seat. She stared at him, an incredulous look on her face. *The scruff ball from the bar?*

Other Girl glared at the interloper. "Stay out of this old man."

Max sniffed. *Old man?*

"This is none of your business."

"Well, I'm making it my business." And he knew exactly what to do. He slithered in close to the young women. He'd done this enough times before, albeit inadvertently, to know that the stink of his alcohol laden breath and clothes would wash over the women in no time.

"Eww, you really stink." *It worked!*

Skinny Girl shoved a hand to her mouth. "I'm breathin' here."

"Get away from us man." Other Girl backed up.

Max chomped on a chip, making a big production out of it. "Don't think so."

They looked at him in disgust.

"Think I'll stay her and talk to my friend." He stood in front of the two women, putting himself between them and the woman in green in the booth.

They clued onto him immediately and their anger surged. They tried to get around him. But he was immovable – and then there was the stink. They took another shot at it though, each girl trying to get around a different side of Max — but they failed miserably. He was just too strong.

Then in a series of flurried and angry attempts to get at the woman in the booth, arms and hands flailed, nails scratched, potato chips flew, the glass of lemonade upturned — but the only thing the young women managed to do, was scrape a bit of skin from Max's forearms and neck and sock him in the chest and face a little.

Katherine didn't know which way to turn. *Oh god.* Or how to help. *Poor guy.*

Max just laughed off their puny hits as they made contact with his body. *Like getting hit with teaspoons.* Though Skinny Girl had a pretty good right hook. Of course he couldn't hit back. They were still women — angry, unreasonable ones — but women nonetheless. And he could never hit a woman.

It was all over in a few seconds, when the bartender stepped in to rescue Max. Then the young women panicked when they saw the bouncers heading their way.

They huffed and puffed, but ultimately slowed to a stop. They weren't getting the woman in green today.

Skinny Girl glared at Max. "What's it to you anyway?"

He erupted with a sly grin. "I'm here with her." He nodded towards the woman in green.

Skinny Girl unleashed a sarcastic sneer. "Yeah right. You're with her — my arse."

Katherine wanted to melt into the seat.

"What? You don't believe me?" He then sent a hopeful look in Katherine's direction.   "Tell them honey."

Katherine bared her teeth – she was going for a smile – but it might have just been a slow nod.

Max frowned and turned back to the girls who had now untangled themselves from his hold. "So you see? How could she be with your moronic boyfriend if she's here with me?"

They stopped, stunned into silence. "Oh." Not sure they still believed it. "Well if that *is* the case…sorry then."

But their apologies came too late. The bouncers steered the girls outside, and the bartender came back again for a second time to clean up the mess.

Max flashed him a mischievous grin. "I thought you said this was an upmarket establishment." Looks like for once he wasn't the biggest trouble maker in the bar – on the contrary.

The bartender just smirked and left. He didn't usually have so much trouble.

Finally alone, Max ventured a look over at the woman in green. He raised an eyebrow. "Eventful night huh?" He placed what was left of the glass of lemonade in front of her. Then in a sudden movement, he bent down and picked up the paper umbrella off the seat and popped it back in the glass. "This was for you."

It looked pitiful – even the umbrella was busted.

Katherine looked at the man in front of her and his pathetic offering. But there was something so humble and kind in what he'd done, protecting her from those women like that, that she didn't have the heart to tell him to go.

Unbelievable, even to herself, she found herself saying to the flannel-clad, goatee-sporting, roughhouse man in front of her, "Please…sit down."

Max beamed. A twinge of happiness fluttered inside him. He eased himself down onto the seat opposite her in the booth, and held out a greasy, salty hand. "I'm Max."

She flashed a quick smile back at him and took his hand. "I'm…." She thought about it – then looked him straight in the eyes and decided. "Kat."

His eyebrows shot up. "Like…kitty?"

She examined him with comical eyes. Then she laughed – it was unexpected, loud and long – a genuine belly laugh. It was as if all the stresses and worries of the past couple of weeks rode the waves of laughter right on out of her. *Man that felt good.*

Max joined in – not sure what he was laughing at, but her laughter was infectious – or maybe it was the alcohol – it didn't matter.

When she stopped laughing, she turned her attention to Max, and looked at him with the most serious eyes which told him. *I've got something very important to tell you.*

"Max." She leaned in closer encouraging him to do the same.

His face heavy with expectation. *Might be getting somewhere here.*

Then she delivered her message. "You really do stink." Her laughter burst out of her again in fits and starts. Tears streamed down her cheeks as she waved a hand in the air at the hilarity of the situation.

Max had stopped laughing a while back. He wasn't

sure what the right response was. *Women.*

He toyed with the empty glass and subconsciously tapped it towards Kat. He waited for her to get a grip.

But she couldn't – she was practically in hysterics. Everything was funny and the sight of the busted umbrella didn't help. When she finally regained control of herself, she said, "I'm sorry Max. I'm not usually like this." She sniffed. "God, I needed that."

Speechless, Max just sat there, faked a smile. *Women.*

Chapter Twelve

The bartender swiped a cloth across the already clean bar top, then stared out over the room, surveying his charges. That's how he liked to think of them – especially when they were drunk, or on their way to it. He was responsible – and he'd seen it all in here. People never ceased to amaze him. The things they did and said with a gutful of grog.

Take the couple he was glaring at now sitting over in the back booth. He shot daggers at the smelly, unkempt 'Max' – he'd said his name was – and the beautiful, classy vision in green. He huffed. *Unbelievable.*

"Beauty and the beast." He muttered to no-one.

His eyes glanced back and forth between the two unlikely acquaintances, then stopped again on Max. *How did he do it?* It certainly wasn't the typical pairing of the patrons. But he had to believe it, since he'd watched their unorthodox meeting with his own eyes. *White knight syndrome.*

Max had saved the woman from the wrath of a

couple of young interlopers. The bartender screwed up his nose at the thought. He'd tried to get their first, but Max beat him to it. Still, he had to hand it to the guy. He took a fair pounding from the women – *especially that skinny chick – she was really hooking in.*

He watched Max flip a pink umbrella on the table. He smirked at the recollection of his petty attempts to make Max look silly. Jerky thing to do, but a moment of jealousy had stung him. He listened more intently than he should as he watched Beauty peel out another burst of laughter. But he didn't see what was so funny. *Bet that guy has a lot of jokes in him.*

Max laughed out loud. He was having the time of his life. He'd joked and laughed and giggled – well Kat did the giggling – talked and swapped the occasional deep and meaningful anecdote for the best part of two hours.

It was one of those meetings where you meet someone for the first time without expecting it, you talk for hours – with no pretences, just being yourself – then you can't remember a time when you didn't know them. *Wow, had he ever felt like that?* Don't think so. But he liked it.

He'd told Kat all of his best clean jokes that were sure to impress. He could tell that she was a clean jokes kind of person. *Better save the sicko jokes for the boys back home.*

He chuckled as he thought of another one. "So this guy goes up to a chick in a bar and says, 'you must be from Tennessee?'"

Katherine grinned like a schoolgirl, anticipation glistening in her eyes. "No."

Then he brought it home. "Because you're the only ten I see."

She squealed out with laughter. *I'm an eight – but whatever.* Then instantly flung a hand over her mouth. *God what was she doing? She was out of control. This wasn't her.* If Steven could see her now. She felt the rush of excitement – the guilty pleasure – of behaving out of character. The jokes were terrible, but for some reason she found them hilarious.

Max smiled to himself. *Lame, but she's buying it.* He had a new audience for his well-used jokes. *Fresh meat.*

"So, this man comes home to find his wife in bed with three other men. He says, 'Hello, hello, hello, what's going on here?'"

Kat shook her head at him – her cheeks hurt from laughing. But she wanted the punchline.

"So the wife says, 'What – aren't ya talkin' to me?'"

She squeezed out another laugh. *Stop it, she couldn't take anymore.* She'd never laughed like this before. *And fun!*

"Max, you're a hoot." She wiped a tear from her eye. "God I'm going to get laugh lines." Then she tried to sound serious. "Thank you Max."

"For what?"

She smiled with genuine appreciation in her eyes. "You've been a real tonic."

"Well that's a new one. I've been called a lot of things before-" He cut himself off. A pang of disappointment stabbed him. He suspected being called a tonic was not a woman's way of indicating a romantic interest. *Probably wasn't going to get laid tonight.*

But then it hit him that he'd stopped thinking about

trying to get laid a couple hours or so ago. *Wow. That's a turn up.* He'd been so distracted by their conversation and the fun they were having, that he'd forgotten to break out his best moves – his real moves – and lay them on her.

It felt like a lifetime ago since Max had swooped in to save the day, foiling the attack on Kat by the two young women in sheaths. He'd gained her confidence – somehow.

God the luck of it. Sitting here in the booth with the absolutely gorgeous Kat, getting along as if they'd known each other a lifetime. He guessed saving her life – well at least saving her from a few nasty scratches – had done the trick.

Guess she thought he wasn't all that bad since he was brave enough – or stupid enough – to put himself in the line of fire the way he did. In any case, she'd thanked him, and said he could sit while she waited for her friend to arrive.

Time had melted away before they realised they were still waiting for her friend to arrive. *In fact, so was he – Baldo hadn't turned up yet either.*

But the two new friends were having a blast, still rooted to their spots on opposite sides of the booth. Neither one was making a move to leave. The pub had been hopping with the evening crowd for some time now, but they were oblivious. It was just white noise – inaudible to them. They were in a bubble – the Max and Kat bubble.

Katherine couldn't remember the last time, if ever, she'd talked so openly with a man. She hadn't looked at Max as a possible suitor, and wasn't trying to impress him. Maybe that was why she felt so free. *She was talking to a friend* – uncomplicated by romantic liaisons.

She didn't need to convince him of how clever she was – didn't need to recite her resume. And she didn't need to constrain her behaviour. In fact, restrictions were out the window – apparently. No topic seemed to be off the table. She could talk to him – really talk to him.

In this world she was in with Max, she was free from the binds of propriety and prudishness. She plonked her elbows on the table and leaned in towards him, her hands resting under her chin – a thoughtful pose.

"So Max, what are you going to do now that you've been fired for being horrid to women." She laughed. Private joke between them – he got it.

"Well, believe it or not, I'm writing a book."

Her eyebrows hitched up a notch. "No."

"Yes princess. A book."

She giggled. "What kind of book?" *Fishing 101? How to Fix an Outboard?*

"Erotica for women." He blurted.

Her eyes ballooned, her stare fixed. "What?"

Max nodded slowly. *Yes.*

"Really?"

"Really." But as he said the word, his meeting with jerk Johnson the publisher came to mind. "Yeah, pitched it to a publisher this morning."

"And…?"

"He hated it. Said it was all wrong – that it wasn't really for women."

He watched as his new friend kept a still pose –

staring right into him.

"You wrote an erotica book?" Her eyes still wide and edged with disbelief.

He cringed. "More like a couple chapters." He took a sip of his beer. "Needs work – apparently." He looked down at his drink, trying to hide his disappointment.

But Katherine caught it.

She whispered. "Can you keep a secret?"

He boomed. "No, I'm a leaky vault."

She cracked up laughing again. Then when she calmed down she asked again. "No seriously. Can you keep a secret?"

"Ok." Max shrugged. He leaned in ready, attentive, listening.

Her eyes darted around – *no-one listening* – she raised a hand around her mouth to protect her secret, then she mouthed the words with hardly a sound. "I-read-erotica-books."

She nodded with her eyebrows to reinforce the point. *God did she just admit that out loud?* If only Sally could hear her now.

Max cupped his hand around his mouth in the same manner and mouthed his response back to her. "I-don't-care." And shook his head to reinforce the point.

Kat flung back in her seat, bumping against the wall, and burst into another round of laughter. *God she was so out of control.* Then she sat up stiff and straight as a sudden doubt stabbed her – *she shouldn't have told.* Then in order to mitigate her confession she added. "But just for research…for work you know."

Max sneered as he squinted a doubtful eye at her. "Research my arse. Admit that you read them for pleasure." He waved a finger at her as if she was a naughty child. "Don't tell fibs Kat."

She burst into laughter once again. She couldn't hold it in. "You're right." Swiped away another tear. "I do enjoy reading them." Then she hastened to correct. "Not all of them though – not the real sicko ones."

He frowned at her.

The laughter died away for a few seconds and they found themselves still looking directing into each other's eyes.

Katherine cleared her throat.

Then as if the same thought struck them simultaneously, they glanced at their watches.

Katherine furrowed her eyebrows. "Hey, didn't you say you have a friend coming to meet you."

"Yes I did." Max realised that he hadn't heard from Baldo. "But he's obviously not here yet." He looked up at her. "Are you trying to get rid of me?" He frowned. "Am I not entertaining you enough?"

He picked up a cardboard coaster off the table, ripped a piece out of it and stuck the remaining coaster across the bridge of his noise, it held firm. Then he swung his head around. "Who the fuck is throwing coasters?"

Katherine laughed out loud. "Do people tell you that you're an idiot…a lot?"

"As a matter of fact princess, I've got a friend that does…yes. And he's the one that's not here yet." He pulled the coaster off his nose. "You'll meet him when he gets here. In fact, I think you two would get along really well." Max heard what he just said. *What the hell did he say that for? He didn't want to set Kat up with Baldo. He saw her first.*

She chuckled. Her voice soft and inviting. Then her smile vanished. *Sally!* She remembered her own friend. She hadn't heard from Sally either.

They both checked their phones.

Max read one of the texts from Baldo. *'Delayed – might have to meet you back at the hotel.'*

Sal's voice mail message on Katherine's phone said, *"Kat. Almost there."* She checked the time of the message – thirty minutes ago. She instinctively flung a look towards the doors. But no-one entered.

She drew her eyes back to the man sitting in front of her. Max was still reading his friend's text messages. She snuck a look. He definitely was a harsh looking man, no doubt about it. But there was something about him – something honest, something raw.

She couldn't believe she'd only known him for a few short hours. Maybe it was just all the gaiety talking, or the gratitude she'd felt when he'd protected her earlier, but she had to admit, she felt a warmth inside of her when she looked at him – *a sort of closeness. Why would she feel this?* This was not a potential suitor – not even close – and for the entire evening that's not how she'd thought of him. He ticked none of her boxes – *absolutely none of them.*

And yet, she felt like she knew Max. She could see who he was – there was no façade to get through, no confusion about who he was, or what he thought. He was an easy book to read. Max had a welcome mat out.

And she was standing on it. She looked puzzled. *Why was she standing on it?*

She supposed he wasn't really that bad on the eyes. His sandy-brown hair was light and breezy – though it looked like it'd been combed by hand – his hazel-green eyes drew you into him, especially when he smiled. He was cheeky, a larrikin, and she was surprised to admit that she found him quite endearing – really.

She thought about the way he'd told his lame jokes – the way he put himself out there with his opinions – as if he really wanted to share some of himself and he genuinely seemed to want the people around him to enjoy themselves. *Well he certainly accomplished that.*

Ok, maybe to an outsider, it probably looked like a lame ploy to win over a woman, but in her current heightened state of laughter-induced euphoria, she admitted that she thought him quite selfless and caring.

She moved onto his tangible assets. She could see why another woman might look at him in a romantic way. *Well maybe not romantic.* But maybe sexually. His body was strong and fit, a little taller than average, clearly weathered from years of hard manual work, but still held a youthful promise. *Particularly after he showered,* she presumed.

She didn't notice the smile playing on her lips, as she remembered Max's words from earlier in the night – *"worked hard, partied hard"* – *he sure looked like that was true.*

She gave herself permission to gaze at his forearms as he tapped the phone pad. She could see the muscles moving as he tried to operate the tiny buttons. *Who wouldn't want to be wrapped up in those arms?* Those big, strong, arms probably capable of lifting her small frame like a feather. She felt an unexpected shot of excitement. *God what was she thinking?*

But as quick as the thought struck her, it was gone, replaced by a sudden pang of sympathy for him. No, she could not think of him that way. He was just too far off the mark from her checklist – he was off the charts off her checklist.

She watched him reading his messages. *He really was raw.* But then he was definitely an experience – an acquired taste. She smiled. *Wonder what Sal would think?*

Max suddenly looked back up at her. He lowered his eyes. "What are you thinking about there princess?"

She blushed, and straightened in her seat, hopelessly attempting to cover the fact that she'd been eyeing him off.

He raised an eyebrow at her. *I think she was checking me out.*

"Oh…ah." *Quick! Cover story.* Then a thunderbolt hit. "I was just thinking…can I read that manuscript of yours?"

He flopped back in his seat. "Ah…I guess so." He realised this implied further contact after they left the pub tonight – or maybe later tonight.

Katherine just realised the same thing. *Oops.*

Max grinned to himself. *Wow. That was unexpected.* He was surprised.

Frankly…so was Katherine.

Sally burst through the doors of The Upmarket Bar,

wild eyed, and flustered. She stood panting inside the doors, eyes darting around the room searching for Kat. She expected to see her housemate waiting quietly in a corner, absorbed in her reading.

And since she hadn't received any hurry up texts or messages from her – or any messages at all for that matter – she figured Kat mustn't be too mad at how late she was. *Bus problems, Kat would understand.* She took the bus instead of driving in, because Kat still had her car in the city – they'd drive home together.

Sal scanned the room – *nice place, lives up to its name.* She grinned. Typical Kat – even her choice of pub was conservative. The patrons were pretty respectable looking. It was busy and hopping, but still perfectly bearable and serene. *Except for that under dressed yobo over there and his raucous girlfriend. Wait….*

Her eyes zeroed in on the girlfriend in the green dress. *Kat?*

She watched as Kat threw her head back with laughter – *so animated.*

"Katherine!" She stared in horror. Then a sudden thought – *was Kat in trouble?* Then she looked again. *Didn't really look like it.*

Katherine's ears perked up – a familiar voice.

"Katherine," she said it again.

She heard it again. It was coming from the direction of the door.

Katherine looked up, then beamed out a smile at her friend.

Max turned his head to see the buxom blonde in the short dress with her mouth open. He raised an eyebrow at Kat. "That's your friend?"

She nodded and waved Sal over – a big Cheshire grin on her face.

Sal glared. The man with Kat must have said something funny, because Kat's head just flung back again in another fit of laughter. *God is she flirting with him? Clearly not in trouble then.*

Sal sauntered over with an uneasy swag, then pulled up, standing over them. Her eyes questioning.

Katherine stayed put in her seat. "Sal, this is Max." Then she looked at Max. "This is-"

"Sal." Max cut her off and took over, a big smile on his face. "It's nice to meet you." He stood and offered his hand to shake, almost toppling over.

Sal didn't take his hand. "Are you drunk?" She directed the question to both of them. Then a thought hit her. *Has Kat ever been drunk?*

Max blurted out a response. "No, just me. Guilty. Plastered."

And indeed he was. Sal reared back at the stench of body odour and stale beer. *Good god.*

She gave Kat a 'what are you doing with this guy look'. Then glared at Max.

Her attention turned back to Kat, her voice flat. "I'm sorry I'm late."

Max eyed the blonde vision in the short, tight dress. Alluring curls bobbed around her neck. She was sexy – very sexy.

"Sally?" Kat gave her friend a 'don't be so rude' look. "Aren't you going to say hello to Max?"

Sally cocked her head at him, her eyes shot suspicious daggers. "Hello. Max."

Max thrust his hand out towards her again. She

took it this time with more than a mild level of reluctance.

"Sally." He pumped her hand. "Kat's told me all about you."

Sally cringed at the fresh waft of stale beer and chips emanating from Max. *How can Kat be standing this?*

"Ah…yeah…Max. Nice to meet you too." She lowered her eyes. "Kat. Can I talk to you for a second?" She pointed towards the bar. "Over here."

Katherine offloaded a few stray giggles and rose to stand. "Sure Sal." She shuffled out of the booth. "Excuse me a minute Max." She put a hand on his shoulder.

Her friend's eyebrows shot up, and she all but dragged Kat by the elbow to the bar. Her friend had to quick step to keep up.

The bartender watched from afar, curiosity mounting at the sight of another party joining the duo.

"Sal, what's the rush?"

Sally pulled Kat into a huddle facing the bar – she didn't want Max to hear what she had to say.

"Kat." She practically hissed, though she was aiming for a loud whisper. "What are you doing?"

Katherine's head lurched back in surprise. "What do you mean?"

"That guy is terrible!" She pointed in front of her friend, but left no doubt that she was indicating Max.

Katherine was still smiling, barely acknowledging her friend's concerns.

Sal scowled. "Snap out of it will you, I'm trying to talk to you."

"Yeah Sal I know. But what are you taking about?"

"What do you mean what am I talking about? Who is he? Why are you talking to him? I'm sure I saw you flirting."

She was flirting with Max? Ok, so maybe she had been.

"Kat!"

"Sorry Sal. It's just Max." She giggled again at the thought of him.

Sal was beside herself. "What do you mean 'just Max'? You say that like he's an old friend." She screwed up her face and shook her head. "Kat, he's a stranger." As hard as she tried, her whispers weren't really whispers anymore. "You've known him for a minute!"

Kat laughed. "More than two hours." She corrected and held up three fingers to illustrate.

Sal stood back and looked at her friend as if she'd never seen her before. "Kat have you been drinking?"

"What? No. Of course not." She hissed and frowned.

"Then what are you doing with this guy?"

Katherine placed a hand on her friend's shoulder. "Sal, stop worrying. It's fine. He's funny."

"Funny!" Sal squeaked out. "Kat." She looked over at Max and shook her head. "What's gotten into you? This isn't you. This isn't a nice guy."

Katherine pointed a finger at Sal and spoke in a measured tone. "I thought you didn't want me to date nice guys. You were the one who told me to try something different."

Sal's eyes bulged. "I meant a different guy – not a different species!"

Katherine could only smirk. *That was funny.* But it

did make her think. That was a really good way to describe Max – so different from other guys she'd known. He really was like a different species of man.

Sal was still blabbering on. "Ok, yes I wanted you to ditch Steven. But Kat it's one thing to make a few changes in your choice in man, but this guy…." She couldn't contain her exasperation. "The pendulum's swinging back to the other end of the spectrum here."

Katherine laughed. "Get a drink Sal. You're mixing your metaphors again." She grinned and spoke quickly. "And stop worrying will you. I'm not dating him. He's just a friend. Look, come and meet him properly. We're going back to his hotel soon."

"What?" Her voice an octave above a squeal. She took a dramatic step back and looked her friend up and down. "Who are you? And what have you done with Katherine?"

Katherine belted out a hearty laugh. "She's still here – just has her eyes open a bit more. Look I'm having fun. Isn't that what you told me to do?"

"Yes, I wanted you to lighten up a little. I didn't want you to go crazy." She was almost hysterical.

Still laughing. "He's not that bad really." *God something just feels so different, so liberated.* "Look, I admit, I wasn't sure at first either. But I'm telling you Sal, there's something different about him."

Sal frowned. *Yes, his clothes, his smell, he's crude.*

"Stop frowning Sal. You'll get frown lines." She laughed. "Come and sit with us and get to know Max a little. I promise you. You won't be disappointed."

***

Katherine was right. Sal did sit with them and eventually calmed down, and she had to admit, Max wasn't as bad as she'd first thought.

He'd won Sal over, just as Katherine knew he would.

However…that was small consolation for the predicament they found themselves in now. They had left the pub close to half an hour ago, and that's about how long it had taken them to get the very drunk Max – because Max kept on drinking – out of the pub and along the few streets that led back to his hotel.

The plan had originally been to wait with Max at the pub until his mate got there, but his mate never arrived. So they were stuck with him.

They tripped and staggered along the carpeted hallway – heels sticking – towards Max's hotel room, each under one of Max's arms, acting as human crutches, and leading the barely functional Max towards the front door.

Sal grinned, a little tipsy herself by now. "Good pick up Kat."

Katherine burst out a laugh. Her friend wasn't the only one who'd been surprised tonight. This is the last thing she thought she'd be doing when she broke off her relationship with Steven – *just a few hours ago.* It seemed like an eternity.

Sally grumbled. "His mate should be doing this."

They heaved Max's body against the door and ferreted around his pockets for the key.

Sally pouted. "God this is terrible." She held her breath. Because if there was any part of Max that didn't stink before, it did now. "He can't even stand up. You know, we could roll him right now and he wouldn't even notice."

Katherine tried to scold her friend, but only managed a broken laugh. "Stop making me laugh Sal, or I'll lose all my strength and drop him." She chuckled at her own weakness, still high on life. *This was crazy.*

"Trust me, he wouldn't feel it." She rolled her eyes.

"Stop it Sal."

"Well, what happened to his mate? He was supposed to be here hours ago."

"Stop whining will you." Katherine snickered. "You found his key yet?"

"Yeah." Sal held it up and jiggled it – a plastic card with the door number on and a key attached. *Bit old fashioned. Didn't think they still had these in the city.*

They succeeded in getting Max through the grey hotel door. He stumbled, but they gripped onto him and stopped him from falling flat. They let the door swing shut behind them, satisfied only when they heard the clunk of the lock.

"The bed." Sal pointed.

The brown quilted, queen size bed took up most of the space in the room. A small kitchenette barely qualified as a separate room.

They half dragged, half walked, Max towards the bed, then laid him down on it with a plonk.

"Thank God." Sally moaned stretching out her arms. "He's heavy. Think I pulled a muscle."

Katherine smirked. "Yep." *He was heavy. Probably all those muscles she was checking out earlier.*

"And he still smells something shocking." Sal's voice high pitched again.

"Yep." Her friend giggled. She couldn't seem to come down off her high.

They flopped down on the bed next to Max, and breathed heavy, exhausted breaths.

A silent moment passed. They kicked off their heels.

"You know you surprised me tonight Kat." Sal was calm again.

"Yeah? How so?"

She waved a hand like a wand over the sleeping Max. "I didn't think you had something like this in you."

Katherine shook her head. "What do you mean? Meeting Max or getting him here?"

She narrowed her eyes and grinned. "Both."

"Well, neither did I, I guess." She sighed. "It's funny Sal. Sitting there, talking to Max tonight, I've never felt so free. I don't know…maybe it was a just a knee-jerk reaction to calling things off with Steven. But I honestly had such a great night. I've never laughed so much."

"Yeah I know." *He was kind of funny.*

They both sighed.

"Now what?" Sal asked, looking around the room. "Do we just leave him here."

Katherine glanced around the room, her interest suddenly peaked – *surprisingly neat.* A few clothes were unpacked on the far end of the bed near a small overnight bag – very humble clothes, very humble bag. It looked like Max had been trying to pick out his best pair of shorts. Katherine put a hand over her heart. She found the humility of Max's suitcase and belongings quite touching. He was no fancy man.

Sal saw the same thing. "You're right." Her voice soft. "He is different."

Katherine smiled – *I told you so.*

"He's unpolished." She added. "But he is real."

"Come on, let's get his thongs off him and get him tucked him."

Mission completed. *Now what?*

Sal wiggled an eyebrow. "You know we could do anything to him and he wouldn't know."

"Don't even think about it Sal. Leave him alone."

"Come on, I was just kidding." She waved away the notion – but her eyes sparkled just a little bit too much. She pointed to Max. "I can't believe this drunkard is your dream guy."

"I wouldn't go that far Sal." She frowned. "But he is ok."

"All right. So what now?"

"Guess we leave huh?"

"We could do that." A mischievous grin crept over Sal's face as she walked over to the small, round coffee table. "Or we could read this." She yanked out a small, grubby manuscript from underneath a flannel jacket. She waved it about, teasing.

Katherine's eyes were saucers. She knew immediately what it was. "We couldn't."

"Yes we can Kat. Didn't you say he offered to let you read it?" She flipped the pages, eager to get to it. She started reading before Kat could stop her.

Katherine launched herself across the room. "Well." She snatched the document from her housemate's hand. "That means only I have permission to read it."

She had to admit, she wondered what a man like Max thought about women, sexually.

Katherine held the manuscript between her two palms. *Not very big.* She flipped it open to a page that had been tagged with a red sticky note. *Must have been of particular interest.* Then she started to read.

'Tara took Rock's 'thermometer' in her mouth. She rolled her tongue under the helmet's ledge, taking care to pay special attention to every groove edge. She was determined to please him.'

Jesus. Katherine winced. *This is terrible.* But she kept reading.

'Rock looked up at the ceiling. *God this feels good.* Then Tara started sucking, with what felt like the strength to suck a golf ball through a garden hose.

Rock looked down to the sight of the top of Tara's head. He took a firm hold of her hair as she moved, gently holding her head in place.

He became breathless. "Don't forget." His voice was barely audible as the pleasure threatened to consume him. "The good girls swallow."'

Katherine tossed the manuscript onto the floor. *Disgusting!* She knew why the publisher rejected it. It definitely wasn't written for women. *Maybe she was wrong about Max after all.*

"What is it?" Sal asked with an eager expression on her face. "Is it good?"

She didn't answer.

"Come on Kat, you're killing me, what does it say?"

Katherine held up a hand like a traffic guard. She stared at the manuscript laying sprawled on the floor. Thoughts of the man she'd met at the pub and the hours they'd spent getting to know each other flashed like a movie trailer in her mind. *Was he a chauvinist? Maybe he was fired from his job for good reason?*

But then she remembered the way he'd leapt to her defence, the injuries he'd taken for her, the way he'd made her laugh. He was one of the good guys. *Wasn't he?*

Decision made. She'd give it another chance. Besides, her curiosity was peaked. *Maybe it gets better.* She scurried over, then picked up the manuscript between two fingers as if it had been dipped in mud, and carried it back to the small table and sat down.

Sal watched the carry on. *All very dramatic. Can't be that bad.*

Katherine flipped a few more pages in the stack, screwed up her face, braced herself and read a few more lines. She saw that the amenable Rock Hard was now preparing to 'get busy' with Tara.

Katherine cringed, chided herself for what she was about to do, but she read on.

'After allowing Tara the pleasure of servicing his manhood, Rock wanted to return the favour.

"Lay down." He commanded and pointed.

She obeyed. She walked over to the super soft blanket spread out so thoughtfully on the floor near the fireplace and lowered herself down onto it.

Rock watched her for a moment. The lights were dimmed in the room and he could see the fire dance in her eyes. He took a step towards her. "Take off your panties."

Tara's heart beat faster and a warm flush settled over her. She'd wanted this all night. She did as she was told. She was still fully dressed except for her panties. She lay back, her dress starting to slide up her thighs.

Rock walked slowly towards her, savouring the dominating role he'd put himself him. He knew women liked to be dominated.

He kicked off his shoes on the way. Then knelt down beside Tara. He reached out and pushed a cushion gently under her head.

"Thank you." She whispered.

Rock moved into position between her knees. He ran a hand over the soft skin on her thigh.

She shivered and let out a quiet moan of anticipation. Then as if in a sign of gratitude to Rock for the gift she was about to receive, she said, "Are you sure?"

His droll response quelled her concerns. "Don't worry baby. I've done this before. No muff's too tough."

Then he advanced quickly, locking onto the forbidden zone like a suction cap on a window.

She called out with excitement.

He commenced the task at hand. Out of respect, he held back his dry reaching for the first couple of licks – *have to hold on to give her some pleasure.* He was licking like a thirsty cat – aimless and desperate – he knew he had to hit all the right spots.

Then when he thought he had given her enough, *at least eight licks should do it*, he suddenly raised himself up, grabbed hold of her hips and deftly flipped her over.

Her look of surprise and excitement caused an urgency to pump through his veins. *He knew it was important not to kill the moment by losing momentum.*

He hastily encouraged Tara to her hands and knees – doggy style. He moved in quickly intending to strike fast, wanting to maximise her enjoyment after he'd given her oral pleasure. With one hand around his penis, he poked around quickly, found the spot, let go of his penis and he thrust fast and deep.

"Jesus!" she cried out.

Rock smiled. *She loves it.*

He rammed into her, breaking only briefly to let her know how much she pleased him. "Fuck you feel good baby!"

Tara gripped the blanket, the cushion flipping from her efforts to hang on to something as she easily took him in, again and again…and again. *Fuck it's a big penis.*

Sensing her enjoyment of his ample offering, his pace became more urgent, until one last big heave sent him over the edge.

Tara screamed with delight.

Rock knew he'd made her come, and come hard. Yes, he knew how to please the ladies.

It barely seemed like a minute after they'd finished making love, when it was the next morning. Rock woke to the cool of the morning, the fire was almost out, and the super soft blanket fully covered his body.

He realised they'd fallen asleep on the floor,

exhausted – *and satisfied.*

He rolled over, smacking into Tara. "Baby, you're still here?"

She smiled at him. *Yes she was.* "Yes I am."

He reached out and gently stroked her hair. He loved the way it spread out on the cushion, and looking at her now conjured up memories of last night. He appreciated how she looked when she was down there pleasuring his manliness.

He flung the blanket off and lay there exposed, except for a pair of boxers.

Tara's look of surprise told him everything he needed to know. *She was impressed.* He knew she could see the now familiar massive erection pushing up under the silky fabric.

"Piss fat." Rock explained. "I always wake up with 'em – they're hard enough to crack a flea's back."

Tara's eyebrows shot up.

Rock wiggled his in return with a sexy suggestion. "You wanna fix that for me?'"

Katherine flung the manuscript back to the floor. *Unbelievable!*

Sally's eyes flew open. "Wow that good?"

Katherine shook her head. "That bad." Then she huffed – disappointed.

"Why, what's wrong with it?"

"He's just got it all wrong. The publisher was right. It's not written for women's enjoyment."

But she found it hard to be angry. She looked over at the sleeping Max, snoring, punctuated with the occasional snort. *He tried.*

Earlier that night she thought she could see inside his soul and see him for the person that he really was – flashes of memory, of Max chomping away at a potato chip while saving her from those women in the bar, came to mind. He really was quite gallant in his own way. *He means well.*

She suddenly felt sorry for him. She pitied his real life girlfriends if he thought that was all it took to please a woman. *He's got the intention right, just the mechanics of it all wrong.*

Then an idea struck her.

"Sal!"

Sally jumped.

"I've got an idea."

Sal stood to attention, her blonde curls bounced around. "What?"

"Call down to reception and ask where the hotel's business facilities are. These hotels usually have something. See if you can get us a computer with word, and a printer, oh and some paper."

She crossed her arms. "What are you up to Kat?"

Her friend only offered a smile in explanation. "Just going to return a favour."

"You're not?" She guessed what Kat was up to.

"I am." She flashed a cheeky smile. "Now go…do."

Sal nodded her acquiescence. "Ok." There'd be no point arguing. *Hopefully it wouldn't take all night.* Then as she headed towards the hotel phone, she stopped, rolled her eyes and added an afterthought. "Well I guess it's not like you don't have any experience in this kind of thing."

Sally carried out her friend's instructions to the letter, and before long Katherine was sitting at a computer, new document open and creating some new scenes for Max's manuscript. Her plan was to replace just a few pages – not all of them, just a few here and there to 'tweak' the action.

Hours passed.

"Come on Kat, are you finished? We're never going to get home." She draped herself over a chair, trying to get comfortable on the arm rest.

Another hour passed.

"How much longer? It's almost daylight." Sally ferried over another cup of coffee.

"Not long now."

Another half an hour flew by.

"Kat!" She glanced at the sleeping Max hoping she hadn't disturbed him. *He'd sleep through a freight train in the room.*

Katherine finished tapping at the keyboard, hit print and scooted over to the printer to collect the new pages. She quickly scanned her work, intermittently nodding and smiling. *Yep she was pretty happy with it.*

"Are we there yet?" Sally begged.

"Nearly done." She slotted the pages into place in Max's manuscript.

Sally stood alert now that departure was imminent. She shrugged at the stack. "It's bigger." Then added. "Can we go now?"

"Just have to send a quick email."

Sally groaned. She was beyond tired.

Katherine quickly logged onto her account and tapped out an email, sending it to Johnson, Mars &

Tate Publishing, identifying it as being sent ON BEHALF OF MAX MARTIN, and then she hit the send button.

Max started to stir.

Sally whispered. "Kat, let's get out of here."

They gathered up their bags, slipped on their shoes, left the equipment where it was, and slipped single file over to the door.

Sally was out the door first.

Katherine was close behind, but stopped suddenly. She turned and looked back at the sleeping Max. A pang of regret at leaving him spiked her heart. She blew him a kiss. "Good bye Max. It was nice to have met you."

Then she let the door swing closed behind her, and they heard the clunk once more as it locked back into place.

Chapter Thirteen

Max lay sprawled on the queen sized bed. A white sheet wrapped around his legs. He stirred but couldn't drag himself out of his heavy slumber. His mind a jigsaw of images – a church, a ringing bell – a nightmare.

He looked up to see a massive, chrome bell looming high above him – he was standing under it – and it threatened to fall and swallow him whole. *Why was he standing under a bell?* Then suddenly the bell started clanging, growing louder, its tongue lashing the sides with a violent rhythm.

Max hunkered down, almost lying flat on the concrete floor. He held a protective arm over his head, as if the pathetic effort would stop the bell from falling and crushing him. He heard the sound of his own voice. "Stop!"

But the bell didn't stop.

His head pained, the noise from the bell consumed him. He started spinning, disoriented. Then as quick as the bell had started up, it stopped – it became as soft as a light breeze, then it was barely audible. But Max's ears still pounded in the wake of the noise.

Then the noise of the bell dropped away completely. Replaced by a sound that was thin and tinny. Then Max started to fall, fast and hard, and landed with a thump. He jumped in the bed.

Then he was awake – and the hotel room telephone bleated out a demand.

He ignored it.

Then his own mobile blasted out the Bohemian Rhapsody.

He picked up his phone and flipped it upside down, smacking the end button on the bedside table. He rolled over and groaned. The sheet twisted with him.

Then he heard Queen start up again.

He flopped out an arm and wrenched the phone off the night stand, hit the call receive button and shoved it to his ear, practically biting into it. "What?"

A short pause ensued. "Max Martin?" A smooth business voice enquired.

"Yeah what?"

"Ah…it's Randolf Johnson here."   His voice uncertain.

"Who?"

"Randolf Johnson from Johnson, Mars & Tate Publishing." The spiel rolled off his tongue.

Johnson waited. He was sure Max would remember him from yesterday – *when he slammed his manuscript*. He winced. And hoped the reception he was getting from the other end of the phone would improve.

Max bolted upright and flung off the sheet, kicking the twisted material in a comical fashion off his legs.

The sudden movement made his head throb and his stomach queasy.

Johnson? Yeah he remembered. "The prick publisher from yesterday?"

Johnson cringed into the phone. "Yeah well I guess I was a bit of a prick."

"Uh huh." Max ran a hand over his face. "What do ya want Johnson? Forgot to tell me that I dress like shit too?"

The publisher gritted his teeth before he admitted. "I deserve that."

Yes you do you prick.

"Listen. Max. I'm sorry about yesterday. But things have changed. I'll make this quick. I'm calling to tell you that I've changed my mind."

Max's eyes sprang open. "What?"

"Yes, we like the changes that you sent through overnight. I think we can definitely work with them."

"What are you talking about?"

"The changes Max. The ones you emailed through." He ignored him and kept talking quickly. "Why don't you come back into my office today and we'll discuss it properly." *It was Saturday, but in this business you had to strike while the iron was hot.*

"Mate, I dunno what you're talking about." He ran a hand through his hair, sticking his fingers in the mess.

"Max. Are you listening to me? We want to publish your story. There's some conditions of course. There'll need to be some editing and maybe a little ghostwriting – or maybe a lot – in any case, the point is, we want to publish your book."

Max had nothing but silence to give.

"Max?"

"Yeah I'm here." He rubbed his temples, in disbelief. "Let me get this straight. Yesterday you hated my work – said it was no good, wasn't erotica. Today you're offering me the world." He rolled his eyes even if the prick couldn't see it. "One question – why?"

Johnson blew out a breath. "The changes Max. The ones you sent in last night. We loved them."

"Mate. You've lost it. I didn't make any changes." *I didn't send in any changes, did I?*

He scrounged around in his memories from last night – they were a mosaic at best. He remembered going to the bar – *after his dreams were crushed.* Then there was drinking – lots of drinking of course – which meant he could have done anything.

He glanced around the hotel room. He saw a computer and printer set up on the little dining table in the corner of the room. *Maybe he did make some changes.*

Johnson's voice rang out in his head.

"Max? Are you there?"

He shook his head. "Yeah I'm here." He kept an eye on the computer equipment.

"Look mate, I don't know how you did it, but we really liked what you did."

A sudden sharp rap at the door – Max jumped. He instinctively stood up.

"Max?" the voice in his ear said.

"Yeah, yeah I'm here." His eyes on the door.

"So, today. My office – about twelve noon work for you?"

Another hard whack on the door. Max glared at it.

What the hell?

"Johnson. I gotta go."

"Wait. Do you still have the card Mandy gave you yesterday? With our details on it?"

"Mandy?"

"Yeah, my receptionist."

Max flinched. *Right, the one he tried to flirt his way through to get someone to look at his work.*

He shoved a hand into a pocket on his flannel shirt which he found thrown over a chair. "Yeah I got it."

"Give us a call when you're on your way – I'll order some lunch and will talk turkey."

Max's thoughts scrambled. It was a lot to take in when his head was splitting and his stomach felt like heaving. "Yeah ok. I'll get back to you."

The knocking was louder – more urgent.

He cut the call short. "Gotta go mate. I'll call you later."

He pressed the end button on the phone, took the four steps needed to reach the door, and flung it wide open.

"Baldo! Where the fuck have you been?"

His mate strolled into the room, right past him. "Staying down the hall from you." He frowned. "You would know that if you'd answered your phone even once."

Max rubbed his face and sat back down on the bed. "Oh fuck, sorry mate. Got wasted."

"I figured." He walked over to the window and wrenched open a curtain.

Max groaned and shielded his eyes from the light.

"So what happened?" Gary sat down in a chair and

crossed his legs - tasselled loafers dangled from his feet.

"What the fuck are you wearing on your feet?"

He smiled. "When in Rome." He also had on his city slacks – tan – and a cream shirt. He wanted to look nice. He raised his palms up. "So, what happened to you?"

Max turned and paced, rubbing his temple. "Too much to go into mate. I dunno where to start." He looked up his friend. "What happened to you anyway?"

Gary shrugged. "Nutshell – broke down on the highway – waited for the RACQ – got to the city late, booked into the hotel, then came to see you at the bar. You weren't there – came back here. Left another bunch of messages on your phone, then went to bed."

Max looked at the phone in his hand, and saw the further texts and missed calls from Baldo. "Mate, I'm sorry." He turned and headed into the kitchenette for coffee. He held up the stock standard, hotel white kettle. "Coffee?"

"Nah, had brekky already." He caught Max's frown. "Well I didn't know how long it'd be till I found you."

Gary watched as his mate filled the kettle with water. "So what happened yesterday? Did ya strike out with the publisher?"

"I did." Max looked confused. "At least I did yesterday." He flipped the switch on the kettle and sought out a mug and spoon.

"Is that why you're still in your clothes?" *And you stink.*

Max nodded. "Got plastered."

His mate shook his head and flashed him a

disapproving look. He watched Max shovel a heaped teaspoon of coffee into the mug. He would always be there to pick up the pieces when Max went on a drinking binge, but the collateral damage…well. He wanted Max to get it together – *grow up a bit.*

Max added. "But you wouldn't believe it. Just now – this morning – he rings me. Says he's changed his mind."

"What?" He leapt to his feet. "That's great isn't it?"

"I don't know." He shrugged. "He said he liked the changes I sent him last night. And because of them, he now wants to publish my book."

Gary's eyes grew wide. "You made changes – last night?" He'd never known Max to be able to walk straight when he was drunk, let alone be lucid enough to operate a computer.

Max paced the kitchenette floor, waiting for the water to boil. "I don't think so…I must have I guess. At least that's what Johnson reckons."

"Who?"

"The publisher." He flashed an exaggerated frown. "Keep up mate."

"So you don't remember?"

"Nah." He thought hard about that. *What did he remember?* The last thing that came to mind was Kat and her friend – 'what's-her-name'. "I met these women last night – two of them-"

"Max." His mate cut him off. "I don't want to know." He put his hands up to cover his ears. He frowned at Max, annoyance building. "I'm out there on the road going through shit, and you're getting it on with a couple of women."

"Nah that's just the thing Baldo, it wasn't like that."
He poured the water into his mug and took a sip. "We
just talked. Really talked."

Gary stopped. *That's a new one – and quite unexpected.*
Words he didn't often hear from Max – or didn't hear
ever. He squinted at his mate, studying him. *He did
look genuine.*

He held his hands out in front in surrender. "Ok,
whoever you are – you pussy – what have you done
with the real Max Martin?"

Max bellowed out a hearty laugh. "That's just what
her friend said to her."

"Who?" He was confused. "Who said what to
whom?"

Max slapped his buddy on the shoulder. "I've got a
lot to tell you Baldo." But first, let's go get some
breakfast. That coffee's terrible."

"I've had breakfast."

"Whatever. Well you just sit there while I eat and
I'll fill you in."

Gary chuckled as they made a move to go. Then he
noticed the computer equipment and pointed. "Is that
yours Max?" *It didn't look like Max's usual computer.*
"Did you borrow it from the hotel?"

Max examined the equipment. "No." He looked
puzzled. "I mean I must have I guess." He scratched
his goatee. "I saw it before. Figured that must've been
how I sent the changes to Johnson."

Gary stared at his friend, disbelief etched across his
face. "Max. Do you remember getting here – to your
hotel room – last night?"

Max shook his head slowly. "No." He paused. "Not really mate." He now stared with increased interest at the computer and printer. "I honestly don't know what Johnson's talkin' about hey. Maybe I sent some changes – maybe I didn't."

Max tried to piece together the events of the previous night. "I must have come back here, borrowed the stuff from the hotel like you said."

"Drunk? You did all that while you were drunk?"

Max sighed. "Doesn't seem likely does it?"

"Not really. How did you send the changes to him. Did he say how he got them?"

Yes, Johnson did say. "Ah…emailed them."

His mate scoffed. "Max, do you know how to email…anything?"

He shook his head as if in slow motion, mouth open, like a clown at the show. "No." Then sobriety kicked a home run. "I don't know how to email anything."

His mate nodded at him, his eyes questioning. "Possible someone else did this Max?"

Max snapped his head towards the manuscript sitting on the coffee table. Only it didn't look like the manuscript he'd brought with him. It was thicker – definitely thicker, at least twice as thick.

Gary followed his mate's gaze, walked over and picked up the stack. "Is this it?" He flipped the first few pages.

Max marched over and ripped it out of his hand. "If you don't mind Baldo, I'd like to read this. Why don't you go find a café – I think there's one downstairs, and order us some breakfast?" He held the wad of paper up high. "I'll be down soon."

Gary smirked. "Whatever you say buddy."

Max hadn't let his mate read his work yet. He'd told him that he wanted to make sure it was good enough first. *"You can read it when it's published,"* he'd told him, believing that to be the yard stick by which to measure it's worth. No-one had read it yet and that's the way he'd wanted it.

Then Max stopped in his tracks. *Wait!* A memory sparked. *He'd told Kat that she could read it.*

"Kat!"

"Huh?" Gary turned around.

"Kat wanted to read it." He explained. "I said yes."

His mate glowered at him.

"Yeah yeah I know I said no-one could read it. She asked me." *She was hot.*

Max suddenly realised something else. *That means Kat must have come back to the hotel room with him. Oh god, what happened?*

He glanced around. But there was no sign that she'd been there – of anyone else being there. Just a couple of coffee cups in the sink. He looked at the manuscript in his hands. *Could she have done this? Could someone else? Did he sleep with her?*

He bolted over to a mirror above the table and peered at the disgusting reflection looking back at him. Then he sniffed his shirt. *No, probably not.*

Gary flicked a wave on the way out of the room, but his mate didn't notice.

With clumsy fingers, Max flipped to one of the scenes in the story that he knew by heart – *one of his favourites* – he'd know immediately if there were any changes to that scene – *and whether he'd made them.*

He skimmed over the part where his main character's girl – Tara – the girl Rock Hard had brought home from the club, had just given Rock a blow job. He checked his work for changes, reading over the entire section.

He frowned as he sucked in his lips. He could barely find a trace of his original scene. He read back over the scene again, this time more slowly, looking at the changed words on the page as if they were aliens. He read:

'Rock Hard ushered Tara into his den. She was gorgeous and he felt like the luckiest man in the club when she'd agreed to accompany him back to his home.

He may have only known her for a few hours, but he'd felt an instant connection with her – and he knew that she felt it too. Like two past loves meeting again. There was definitely something special about this girl – an untouched, raw honesty that drew him to her.

As clichéd as it seemed, he was the moth and she was his flame. He was mesmerised, bewitched.

He watched her small, slender figure glide through the doorway then pause a few steps ahead of him. Her auburn hair cascaded down in waves past her exposed shoulders. The faint tips of the tie of her halter-top teased playfully as they darted in and out from under her hair as she moved.

She cast her eyes wide across the room, taking in the exquisite setting. She caught her breath. *Wow.*

"It's beautiful." She gushed, as she tried to take in

every part of the fantasy world he'd created. She watched the flames in the fireplace leap about as if a wind was lightly teasing them. The soft warmth from the fire rose up to take her in an embrace so warm and comforting, she felt the urge to run towards it.

The firelight illuminated the room, its bright shadows danced across the walls. It cast a spell over her. She'd stepped into a dream.

Then she noticed the thick, plush pile rug spread out on the floor just in reach of the fire's heat. "Oh." She felt her heart beat a little faster. The rug was scattered with large white cushions with gold trim. The faint scent of potpourri floated in the air. It was simple but exuded luxury and class.

"You've thought of everything." She blushed a little. She should be angry at his presumption that she would come home with him, but it wasn't in her – not tonight. No, tonight she felt anything but anger.

Her insides churned, and she felt a desire surge – she wanted to lose herself in his fantasy world, to throw reason to the wind. She wanted to be someone else for the evening – someone spontaneous, sexy, and she wanted a man to make love to her – *this man*.

That's why she'd accepted his invitation.

Her eyes flashed coy as she turned and looked at him. "It looks wonderful."

Rock stepped towards her. He lowered his eyes then brought them back up to meet hers. He held her gaze then reached out to take her hands, holding them firmly in his own.

The heat from his hands sent a shiver down her spine. They were strong and demanding. She quivered, imagining what it would be like to be with him – this stranger.

"I'd hoped to meet someone special." He told her, his voice sultry and raw. He waved a hand towards the room. "We don't have to do anything but talk and sip wine till daylight if you like." He smiled, his eyes kind. "Or until we fall asleep. Whatever you want."

He stroked her hair. "I just want to enjoy being with you. I don't care what we do…or what we don't do." He gave her another reassuring smile.

She turned to look at the ivory rug and watched the fire's reflections dance over it. *God it looked romantic –* so warm and inviting. A guilty thought penetrated her consciousness. She imagined how it would feel to be naked on that rug, the feel of the heat from the fire on her skin, caressing her. She imagined how sexy it would feel to have a man – *this man* – inside her, making love to her on that rug right there in front of the fire – completely naked – completely bare – completely exposed.

Her heart skipped a beat at the thought. A twinge of excitement ripped through her body. No, she didn't want to talk all night. And she didn't want to sip wine. And she definitely did not want to fall asleep, not just yet.

Rock watched her with intense desire in his eyes. He watched as she admired the room that he'd created. It was all for her. He watched as the shadows from the fire played across her cheeks, her lips – her soft features angelic under the fire's light. *God she's beautiful.*

If they only had this one night together, then he wanted to give her a night to remember. He allowed his eyes to travel down the length of her slim, tight body, wrapped in a smooth, emerald green, silky fabric that touched all her curves. He felt himself go hard at the sight of her.

He imagined what it would feel like to be inside her, pleasuring her. He throbbed at the thought.

She turned her head and drew his eyes into hers. She reached a hand up to touch his face, as if in answer to his generous offer, ran her fingers lightly down his cheek. It felt smooth – freshly shaven. She shivered. It was the first time she'd touched his face. A thrill rippled through her. Her face flushed hot with need. She was drawn to him. No, she didn't want to talk.

His body strained with yearning at her touch. But he maintained his control. He needed to be sure it's what she wanted.

She slowly reached her hand up and pulled at one of the ties holding up her halter-top. Then she dropped the straps, letting them hang loose over the mounds of her breasts. She took his hand in hers and placed it on her breast.

It's all the sign he needed. He drew her top up over her arms then let it fall to the floor. She gasped as the cool air hit her body. She was exposed, standing in front of him.

He took her hand and led her within the fire's reach. The fire's soothing touch warmed her skin, then it started to heat up the air around her. She unzipped her skirt, and dropped it to the floor, then gently pushed it away with her shoe.

Rock groaned with need at the sight of her standing in front of him wearing only her bra, panties…and heels. An urge tugged at him, pushing him to move towards her. He fought to keep control. *Not yet.* He badly wanted to lay her down on the rug and take her right there and then. He was hard again. She was more beautiful and sexy than he'd imagined. Her curves were sexy, her breasts full and wanting. He couldn't wait to be inside her.

He watched her with hunger in his eyes as he shed his socks and shoes, peeled off his cream jacket and shirt, unbuckled his belt and slid off his trousers, leaving him standing in front of her in only a pair of short boxers – and leaving nothing to the imagination.

She gasped, her eyes wide with delight. *God he looked good.* He looked strong, muscles ripped and toned, his chest smooth. He too was on display – exposed – and there was nowhere he could hide the massive erection that strained against the silky fabric of his boxers. *Oh god.* She thought about it – *that was for her* – soon that erection was going to be inside her. She'd feel him filling her up, pleasuring her.

He watched her reaction. He wanted her so bad. He couldn't tear his eyes away from her body. The thin remnants of fabric left on their bodies now were all that was left standing between them and their raging desires. But still he maintained his control, waiting for her sign.

She let her body relax, the room became small and she surrendered to the fire's mercy. She could feel her own need, moist with desire. She reached behind her back and flicked open the clasp on her bra.

Rock watched as her breasts were released from their binds.

Oh god. He wanted this woman bad. The animal instinct inside him was strong and raw. He wanted to run towards her and take her, and take her hard. But he was determined to stay strong, soaking in the feast in front of him.

She let her bra drop to the floor.

Seeing her standing there, wearing only her panties and shoes, drove his insides into a frenzy. He watched as the firelight flicked across her body, taking turns at highlighting her abdomen, her breasts, her face.

He could wait no longer. He was wild with desire. He closed the gap between them – but stopped short of touching her.

She could feel the heat from his body competing with the fire around her. Her eyes pleaded to him. *Touch me.*

And then he did. He put a hand around her waist and drew her into him – their bodies melting into one. The heat between them was electric.

She'd lost control – it felt so hot, so needy, so desirable to be one with his body. *God she could feel him, finally touch him.*

He pulled her in closer, and closed his mouth over hers, drawing her into a passionate kiss. He let his tongue linger to savour her taste, her softness.

She felt the raw power of his tongue caressing, stroking her own. She moaned – she was helpless in his hold. He owned her tonight.

Then without any warning, he lifted her as if she were a feather and cradled her carefully, as he carried her over to the rug. He placed her down like she was a china doll.

Her heat beat faster than she imagined it could. He made her feel like a sexy, desirable woman and she wanted to give him everything she had.

He laid down next to her on the rug. He stroked her hair, then ran a finger down her shoulder. He trailed his fingers down the side of her breast, over her abdomen, and stopped on her thigh.

Her body tingled with the sensation, sending waves of shivers rippling over her. She didn't know how much more she could take – and they'd barely started. *Finish me now!*

But he had other plans for her.

He slowly moved his body over her thighs, and with a soft, steady hand guided her legs till they were nearly pushed down flat against the rug, the straps of her shoes holding firm. She relaxed into the soft, thickness of the plush rug – it felt like velvet against her skin. She'd never in her life felt so sexy, so raw and full of passion.

He traced a hand back up to her hips and slowly started to pull down her panties. Then in a sudden burst, he fisted them in both hands and ripped them apart.

She let out a sharp gasp of shock. Her heart instantly beat hard and fast. So hard, she thought it might burst. *Oh god.*

He groaned. The sight of her auburn bed was exquisite. *God, he had to taste her.*

He touched her thigh gently and coaxed her legs apart.

She shivered – the anticipation overwhelmed her – the fire inside built to an inferno. She flung her head back.

He leaned in towards her centre and gave her a sample of what was to come – he found his mark with his tongue.

She moaned out a guttural cry – moved her legs wider – *more!*

He smiled, pleased with himself. She was all his now. "Don't worry baby, there's plenty more."

He struck again, this time in quick succession.

God she could hardly bear it. Then he pushed his tongue into her, pleasuring every part of her that he could reach. She writhed uncontrollably. He held her legs while he pulled back to pay attention to her clit, which sent her into a wild frenzy. She felt the rawness of his passion for her and she craved a release.

Not yet baby. He played with her for what seemed like forever before he brought her home – her body writhing in sheer and utter pleasure while spasms ripped through her body.

"God, that felt so good." Her voice barely able to form words – her body momentarily sapped of its ability to move.

He let her lay there afterwards for a minute, enjoying the residual quivers from the sensitivity around her clit. *But not for too long.*

He touched the inside of her thigh, to reawaken her sensitivity. "I haven't finished yet." His voice sinfully promising.

He ran a hand down each of her hips, down her thighs, getting into position. He stole a glance at her – he'd left her shoes on and they'd looked so sexy on her beautiful legs. *A little bit naughty.*

He pulled off his boxers and released himself.

She glanced down at him – he was hard – he was big – and he was ready.

"Oh god." She knew what was coming. She leaned back as if to brace for what he would do to her next. Excitement bolted through her. She both feared and wanted it urgently. But she gave herself over to him – trusted him – *do what you want with me.*

He slid on a protective sheath, then moved back towards her centre, then wasted no time – he pushed inside her.

She moaned.

Then he pushed a bit further. It was all he could do to hold out – but he had to make sure she wanted it, enjoyed it.

Her groans of pleasure and anticipation let him know. She arched her back. *More. Please more.*

He pushed harder and then in one continuous thrust, he was completely inside her. She cried out with the immediate feeling of fullness, then as she adjusted to him, she moved to pull him in more.

He punished her by withdrawing slowly.

"Oh god." She knew what he was doing.

Then he plunged back into her. She cried out again. But it felt so good. Each time he plunged hard, he pulled back again, thrusting shallow into her, then ravaging her deep inside. There was no way for her to anticipate which thrust would fill her up again – and her heart beat at the excitement of not knowing, and when it happened, she whimpered with delicious pleasure.

She flung her arms back behind her head. She had

given herself over to him — she'd never felt so good. The pleasure wouldn't stop. She didn't want it to stop.

He caressed her breasts which sent her senses into overdrive. Her body wasn't hers anymore. It was his for the taking.

She lost track of time. When she thought she couldn't take any more, and she was going to release for the second time, she let him know. Her heavy breaths and urgent moans told him.

But he didn't need to be told — he immediately thrust repeatedly, hard and deep.

And then she felt it — the uncontrollable tremors ripping through her very core. They took a long time before they subsided, and when they did, she lay there, bare against the rug, riding out the mini aftershocks that shuddered through her.

She'd never remembered a time in her life when she'd been so satisfied. She felt new again.

She breathed again — a smile of her face. She felt alive.'

Max Martin dipped and raised his eyebrows. A look of surprise had taken up residence on his face for the entire reading. It was as if someone had turned the lights on. *So is this what women want? Is this sex for women?*

If he'd had any residual doubts about whether he wrote this, they'd been shattered. He was pretty sure it wasn't him. *Check that, definitely not him. Nope, didn't write it.*

It's true, he had thought about pleasuring a women like this, but he'd never been quite that thoughtful — and certainly not in that detail.

He felt a pang of guilt stab him. *So that's what it feels like for women?* He thought back to some of his own rushed attempts in real life. A sudden sense of dread enveloped him as he realised that he might not have been doing everything right – *maybe nothing right.*

He paced the floor – no these changes definitely were not something he'd ever thought about – drunk or sober. A quick second thought later – *maybe the drink did it?* Then he shook his head and muttered to himself. "Maybe not."

So if it wasn't him, then who was it? Might have been Kat? Or her friend? Then thinking of the two of them. *Most likely Kat.*

"Probably Kat." He muttered out loud. Then he remembered the emerald green dress on the woman in the rewrite. *Kat was wearing an emerald green dress. Big clue there.*

But why would she do something like that for him? He had to find her.

"Kat who?" The voice startled him. Baldo stood in front of him holding a takeaway breakfast.

"Baldo." He looked up from the manuscript. "Forgot about you mate."

"Well I figured that." He shoved the paper bag of food towards him. "Who's Kat?"

Max shook his head. "The woman from last night." And then it hit him. "You know what? I don't know her last name."

"Well did she leave her number?"

Max frisked his pockets. "I don't know. Maybe she did."

He scoured the hotel room, in case she'd left him

something – anything, any detail at all – but he found nothing. The only item he uncovered again was the business card from Johnson, Mars & Tate Publishing. *Must have been how she knew where to send the changes.*

Then the gut-wrenching realisation dawned on him that he didn't have a way to contact her.

"Maybe she didn't want you to contact her."

"Not helping Baldo." Max frowned.

"Ok. Well you said she had a friend." He gestured with a sweep of his hand. "Do you remember her name?"

He squinted, trying to remember. "No." His voice trailed off. And he couldn't hide his disappointment.

"You met her at the bar didn't you?"

"Yeah." Max clicked his fingers and pointed to his mate. "You're right. The bar. Let's go."

"Now?"

"Yes." Max grabbed the food out of Gary's hand and wrenched a piece of fruit toast out of one of the bags, then shoved it in his mouth on the way to the door. "You can think of a better time?" He spoke between chews.

"Yes." Gary's face was incredulous. "After you've had a shower."

Max halted in his tracks. It *had* been more than a day. He turned back towards the bathroom. "You're right."

***

With Gary in tow, Max pushed through the doors of The Upmarket Bar. It looked different this morning – much lighter and brighter than it was last night. It was quieter, cleaner, and there weren't many people here. *Hardly surprising since it was still not even lunchtime on a Saturday.*

Max had taken his mate's advice and showered and changed – into a fresh pair of shorts and a new t-shirt – wrinkles and all.

He had one mission in mind. He had to find Kat.

His desire to find her had grown stronger since he'd left the hotel. *What a woman – and the stuff she wrote about.* He wouldn't mind trying some of that.

He marched up to the bar full of hope and enthusiasm, and that's when he noticed – *a different bartender.*

"Sorry," the new bartender said after Max gave him his story. "Weekend shift is on now. Can't help you."

"Can you get in touch with the guy that was on last night? He'll remember. Might know something." His face still hopeful. "She might have been in here before – he might know her."

The new bartender shook his head. "Sorry buddy. Personal matter. Policy not to call up staff at home for those types of requests."

Max smacked the bar in frustration. "Look. You don't understand. I met her last night, we got along really well." *I'm not a stalker.* "It's just that she left without telling me who she was."

The new bartender, unfazed by the outburst, let out a relaxed chuckle. "Let me guess." He leaned forward, both elbows on the bar. "She left her glass slipper behind?" He laughed at his own joke. *That one never got old.*

Max eyed him with growing impatience. "When's

the bartender from last night on again?"

"Next weekend. You can come back then and ask if you like."

"What about cameras?"

"You gotta be kidding buddy." He laughed. "We don't let just anyone look at them. Privacy and all that, you know." *You might be a stalker.*

Gary grabbed Max's arm. "Come on mate. You're not going to find her here today."

At a loss, Max turned towards the booth they'd been sitting in. He'd spent what seemed like endless hours in a warm, fun, happy cocoon with her – *Kat*. But everything looked different today – sterile, clean – as if it never happened.

Was it just a dream? He and Kat – Kat *who?* He looked longingly at the table, picturing the beautiful woman in the green, silky dress. He imagined her smiling at him, the way she looked when she laughed, the sparkle in her eyes when she heard one of his lame jokes for the first time.

Kat – his beautiful Kat.

Disappointment dug deep into his heart and sank into the lines on his face. He turned to the door, expecting to see her walk through – like magic. But it didn't happen. She wasn't there.

"Come on mate." His friend was by his side. "Let's go."

Max forced himself to take a step, and then another. But each step felt like a lead weight – because each step took him one step further away – from *her*.

Chapter Fourteen

Max jerked the throttle. The motor revved loud and the boat lurched forward with an instant surge of life.

Gary flung an arm out and grabbed the handle on the centre console. *Damn it Max!* If he hadn't been so quick, he would have landed arse up on the deck.

Max steered the boat away from the pontoon, clearing the boats near the ramp quicker than he should.

"Slow down Max!"

Max ignored him, and sped towards the navigational markers that led the way out of the creek. He pushed the throttle further forward, forcing the boat faster, and sped towards the open water. The motor responded – louder – and the boat surged onwards. Wind rushed past their ears, blowing away all sound along with it.

Gary gripped the handle till his knuckles turned white. The cold, silver handle became his lifeline. His hand strained as he held on during the zigzag Max made around the markers. He hated Max's driving. *Always in a hurry.*

Gary knew Max was a confident boatie – knew every inch of these waters – every sandbank, shallow spot, variation in water level. But he dreaded the days when Max was in one of his moods which seemed to fuel his smash and bash approach to things.

Yes, Max could absolutely be reckless when he was pissed off about something. *And he definitely seemed pissed today.*

"Do you need to be going so fast?" Gary yelled with a touch of desperation in his voice.

But Max didn't hear him – his voice disintegrated in the air.

Max smiled to himself. He knew Baldo had said something. Pretty sure what it would have been.

As they cleared the markers, Max shoved the throttle to full revs. The motor roared unbearably loud till it settled into a deafening hum, drowning out any hope of sound near it.

Jesus Christ Max!

They could see how rough the water was the deeper out they got. It was blowing more than thirty knots – no sane person would come out on a day like today. The forecast was for almost gale force winds. Max peered out at the white caps on the waves – *not quite there yet.* But it was still blowing enough to whip the sea into a frenzy. Definitely a stark contrast to the smooth, calm water they usually came out on.

Max stood at the wheel, feet firmly planted on the deck, eyes glued ahead, polaroid sunnies on, no care in the world – seemingly. Then he saw the black raincloud bearing down ahead. *Crap.* He knew they'd be passing through it soon. He reached down and grabbed the blue rain jacket off the deck. He tossed it to his passenger.

"Here Baldo, put this on." He shoved the jacket at him without looking.

"What about you?" But he knew better. Max rarely wore protective gear on the water. He seemed to be able to withstand any weather in his flimsy t-shirt, shorts and thongs. His uniform.

But not Gary. He shivered, then struggled to don the jacket between intermittent grabs of the handle. "Slow down will you, while I zip this up!"

Max glanced at his mate and pulled back on the throttle, dropping the revs back for a few seconds, long enough to get the job done, then thrust the handle forward again.

He judged the height and angle of the waves as they approached, picking just the right angle to catch the waves side on, rather than punching straight through. On another calmer day, he'd be scouring the water for mackerel. But not today.

He cut the tinnie over some of the waves with ease, but with other waves he had no choice but to punch through, sending the boat airborne then slamming it back into the water. *Like running over big speed bumps in the water.* Max grinned as he checked on his mate.

Gary clung to the handle for dear life. He bent his knees each time the boat hit the water. Max had taught him to do this – *"It lessens the jarring impact from the boat when it smashes back down,"* Max had told him. *Great.*

"We're crazy to be out here!" He yelled at Max.

But all Max heard in the driving wind was, *"Buzz buzz buzz."*

But one look at Baldo's expression, and he received the message loud and clear.

It was early morning, overcast and soon to be raining. The tide had started to turn. Max needed to get to where he was going and back – quickly.

He leaned towards his mate and yelled. "Need to hurry!" He grinned. "Tide's running out and I wanna beat the rain." But he knew that wasn't going to happen.

Then as if the heavens were eavesdropping, the black cloud suddenly exploded over them. Rain pelted down, hard and heavy. And at the speed that they were getting along, the drops felt like pin pricks on their skin.

Gary pulled the hood of the rain jacket over his head, but the rain needles still found their mark on his face and hands. He shivered. He was cold, he was wind-blown and now he was wet. He looked over at his mate. *How the hell can Max stand it?* And more worryingly, *how can he even see ahead?*

Max seemed immune.

"How can you see anything in this Max?" He yelled, his voice swallowed by the rush of wind in their ears.

"Buzz, buzz, buzz."

"Hang on Baldo!" Max strained to see ahead. "Might be some logs in the water up there." He pointed.

Baldo clung tighter – if that was even possible. If they hit a log, it was curtains. *Maybe he should have put the life jacket on too.* Of all the days Max decided to check the crab pots, it had to be blowing a gale – almost –

and raining to boot. Normal people didn't go out on a day like this.

Max pushed the throttle lever to open up full revs again. Now every wave seemed to smash them back down – and harder, spraying saltwater up over the side and hitting them in the face, stinging their eyes. Max shook water out of his ear, felt the salt build up on his skin.

Gary yelled out and laughed at the same time. "You're crazy!"

"You'd be loving this! It's a free exfoliation!" Max retorted, laughing and barely audible to his mate.

Gary frowned. There was nothing to do but grip the silver handle, stare dead ahead and hold on for the ride. If he turned his head, the force of the wind would blow his hood backwards and expose his face again. He guessed Max wouldn't slow down for him a second time.

He was a hostage until Max decided to stop. Unfortunately he was used to this. This was how Max cleared his head – rough, fast and angry. He knew they weren't really checking mud crab pots – oh, Max would make a show of it, but Gary knew what was really wrong. And it had nothing to do with the tide or crab pots. *Katherine!*

No matter how much Max had searched, and no matter how many trips back to the city he'd had – two – he hadn't been able to find her. It had been six months now and he was still pining for his Cinderella.

Max shot an arm straight out, pointing towards an island of mangrove trees.

His passenger's eyes followed. A dirty, white float

teetered in a mangrove tree. A rope dangled from the float and hung all the way down under the surface of the water. *So we're obviously going to stop at a couple of pots then.*

Max yelled into the wind. "Hold on!"

Then he pulled back on the throttle, slowing the boat dramatically. The sudden rush of water around the boat made it sway violently. Max knocked the lever to neutral and let the boat idle.

The wind dropped away, the sound stopped, and all that was left was the ringing in their ears – like walking out of a noisy nightclub for the first time. Their ears needed to adjust.

The rain had slowed to a sprinkle.

"Jesus Max." Gary was relieved to hear the sound of his own voice again.

Max lined the boat up alongside the white float. He pulled the foam ball out of the trees and tossed it into the back of the boat. Then bare-handed, he hauled the rope up like he was moving down a tightrope, hand over hand, feeling for the weight of the submerged pot. The rope became an effort to pull, then with a grunt, Max heaved up the rusty crab pot.

Two big muddies crawled around in the pot. He cracked open the side door and shook the mud crabs onto the deck.

Gary jumped back. "Jesus!"

"Watch out mate." Max warned.

But he didn't need to be told. He scooted to the front of the boat. He may have loved fishing – but he didn't muck about with mud crabs. That was strictly Max's territory. A mud crab had once got him by the finger, as a kid. He remembered how excruciatingly painful it was – *like having your finger stuck in a vice.* It didn't stop until the crab dropped its claw and his dad was able to pry it open to release his finger.

Max put his foot on the back of the crab to hold it in place, then thread a piece of string around the crab, pulling its claws tight in the front.

Gary eyed off the dark green monster. Chills bolted down his spine.

"You want to tie it?"

"Nah mate, I'm fine." He smirked.

He watched as Max secured the crab and tossed it in a bucket then placed a lid on top.

"Chuck us a fish head will ya." He ordered.

"What?" Gary's eyes bulged.

"The bait!" He pointed to a bucket of fish heads at the back of the boat.

Gary thought he might be sick. He gingerly picked up a fish head, blood dripping and tossed it to Max. He watched as Max shoved it down into the bait box – *disgusting, bare hands.*

Max secured the bait box, then balanced the pot on the edge of the boat as he idled along looking for a new spot to toss it back in. When he found the right spot, he hoisted the pot from the edge of the boat, and dropped it back into the water. Then swung the rope and float back up into the mangrove trees.

He then leaned over the side of the boat and rinsed his hands in the salt water and dried them on his shirt. Job done, he flicked the wheel around, and idled along past the bank of mangroves in search of his next pot.

Gary stared out at the water ahead, determined to

make the most of the quiet. "Can't believe it's been six months since you first went to Brisbane to find some sucker to publish your book." He grinned.

Max chucked a fish head at him.

He leaped back. "That's disgusting!"

"Don't be a woman Baldo."

"Why am I even friends with you?"

"Because your life would be meaningless without me." He smirked.

Gary ignored him, and took his place back near the centre console. He was determined to get Max to talk. "Seriously, it seems like a lifetime ago."

Max nodded. He couldn't argue with that. He cut his eyes out over the water – no-one around – as far as the eye could see. *Alone.* Sometimes it seemed like only yesterday when he'd first met Johnson and his book plans took off.

He should probably be a bit nicer to his mate. He owed him – big time. If it wasn't for Baldo, he wouldn't have phoned the publisher back that day – he'd lost interest when his search for Kat failed.

But Baldo had made him do it, and he was definitely glad that he had. Johnson had been serious about publishing his erotica book.

Sure there'd been a lot to do with it since then to get it ready. The past six months had been a whirlwind of activity. He'd easily slipped into a routine with Johnson, Mars & Tate Publishing. He sent them a draft chapter – his style. They re-wrote huge chunks – *from the women's view* – but he was pretty sure they still used some of his ideas.

It didn't bother him that they re-wrote so much of it

– although, it did make him wonder why they needed him at all. *What did they want him for? Must be my great story ideas*, he told himself. He thought his writing had improved – *a little bit* – courtesy of some basic workshops they sent him to, held in the local libraries.

The re-written works had been a lesson for him though. He was shocked by the explicit detail they used to describe how to please a woman – *and how much work it was to please a woman.* Not to mention their 'physical bits' – he'd definitely learned something there.

He often thought back to the first time he'd read the changes Kat had made to his then pitiful manuscript. She'd also shown him what sex was to a woman. He smiled as he remembered her. *Kat.*

"Max, I said it seemed like a lifetime ago."

Max snapped out of his reverie. "Huh? Yeah mate I know." He looked out onto the horizon. "Feels like a lifetime."

He idled along, keeping a close eye on the water level – there was still enough water, but they didn't want to get stuck out there when the tide got too low.

"Things are going well with the book then?"

"Sure are mate." Max's voice lifted. "Book's done. Johnson's happy – that prick." He smirked. He'd actually grown to like Johnson a little bit – *he wasn't all bad, just all business.*

"When's the big release then?" He'd barely asked when he burst out a laugh, as if he'd said the funniest thing he'd ever heard.

"You're nuts Baldo you know that?"

"Nah, I was just thinking. It's unreal to think that you, Max Martin is releasing a book. An erotica book of all things."

Max grinned. "Yeah I know mate. Another two weeks. Can't believe it's really happening." *Thanks to Johnson's ghostwriters.*

"Well you've worked hard on it."

"Rock Hard." They both said at the same time, then laughed.

Gary smiled. "Seriously mate. I'm real proud of you hey."

"Thanks mate." Then he added. "Well I didn't write all the women's bits you know."

"I know." His friend kept his eyes forward. They didn't need to dwell on that part.

"And I'm not making much money from it – it's not what everyone thinks writin' a book hey."

"Yeah I know." Gary nodded. "But you're keeping the wolves from your door. That's the main thing."

Max winked. "Never know, might be a bestseller."

His mate laughed, then a thought struck him. "You gonna ask for your old job back with Frankie?"

"Maybe." He had been thinking about that lately. He did miss it. After all, he was an outboard mechanic at heart – that's what he knew best. "You reckon he'll have me back?"

"Maybe." He chuckled, then added. "At least he can't say you haven't gotten better with women."

Women. He felt as if another black cloud had just dumped its load on him. There was only one woman he wanted to see again. If only he could find her.

"It's a big city Max." Johnson had told him. *"But cheer up. Plenty more fish in the sea."*

But that meant nothing to Max anymore. Not since

220

his serendipitous meeting with Kat – *that's what she'd called it that night* – although he didn't know what that word meant at the time. But looking back, that's precisely how he would describe it. If it wasn't for Kat, none of this would be happening.

Gary shivered, mainly from the cold – but also a little bit from what he wanted to say. He looked over at his friend as if he'd read his mind.

"Sometimes people come into your life for a reason Max. Might be a year, a day, might be an hour." He watched for the expected *'you're a woman Baldo'* reaction from Max – but it didn't come. He kept going. "When that reason is over…then they're gone."

Max frowned at his mate.

Gary snapped his eyes to the deck. "Yeah well I heard that somewhere."

Max had heard it too.

He looked at Gary, then smiled. "You found another sheila yet?"

Changed the subject. He grinned. "No – but I'm workin' on it."

"Uh huh. You want me to set you up?"

Gary glared at him. "Who with?" Then he laughed. "Is there a woman left in this town that will still speak to you?"

Max gave him a sly grin. "Might be soon mate."

"That's true." He smiled. "Thanks, but no thanks. I want a nice woman."

Max fell silent. *Kat was nice.*

Gary was still talking. "Last time I checked, you were all out of nice women." Then he slapped his forehead. "Sorry mate. Didn't think."

Max waved him off. "Don't worry about it mate. I gotta lot of other stuff to think about. Johnson wants me in the city in a few days to do some stuff – paperwork or something. Wants to do a signing when the book is released." His voice raised a half octave as if it was just too much of a surprise. "Here in our home town can you believe it?"

Not really. Gary shook his head. He would never have thought he'd see the day.

***

Barely a week later, Max was in the city again. This time he breezed past the enormous retail shops, ignored them and headed for the open walkway that ran through the middle of the mall.

He breathed in the cool morning air. *Not like the first time he was here – stinking hot.* Today was a fresh, bright winter's morning, and Johnson's office was dead ahead. He smiled at himself. *Definitely getting better at finding his way around the city.*

He ducked across the path in time to miss a hoard of pedestrians striding out towards him. *Still rather be back home.*

Most people he saw were rugged up pretty well. He grunted. *City folk.*

He thought back to the drive here that morning. He'd made good time from home so he'd checked into his hotel early – the same place he always stayed – he was a creature of habit. But if he was honest with himself, he harboured a secret hope – that if he stuck to the same routine every time he came to the city, he might one day find – *her.*

He started across the wide walkway, and tossed a coin in a busker's open case on the way.

His mind flashed back to the first time he'd come to the mall with little more than a scrap of paper and a list of names in his hand, *and a paltry manuscript offering.* It was a Friday back then too, just like today. He still couldn't quite believe it had happened. But here he was, standing in the Queen Street Mall again, and he had business to do with the publisher to finalise details for his upcoming book release – *and signing.*

He slipped into the now familiar corridor, and stepped into the dingy lift. He hit a button in the lift and rode it to the fourth floor. He stepped out and strolled along the hallway – the musty smell hit him – every time. He wished he could drag this hallway out onto the salt water and let it air out. *Would sterilise it too.*

He pushed through the glass doors at the end of the hallway, and glanced over at the tall, wooden reception counter. A young, dark haired, hazel-eyed girl looked up at him. She smiled – warm and welcoming.

"Max!"

Max strolled up to the counter. "Hey Mandy."

"How are you?" Her eyes were bright. "I heard you were coming in today."

He flashed a sincere smile in return. He'd grown fond of Mandy. He brushed away the lingering embarrassment from his clumsy and obvious efforts to flirt his way in to see Johnson all those months ago. Knowing her better now, he felt like an idiot.

"I'm good." He acknowledged her question.

She waved a hand towards the wooden door on her left. "Ran…ah…Mr Johnson won't be long. I'll let him know you're here." And she did. She buzzed him.

"Are you looking forward to your first book signing?" She flicked her fringe out of her eye.

Max leaned on the counter – that same wooden counter where it had all started. "You know what Mandy? I really am." *Did he really believe that?* "Are you going to be there?"

She grinned. "Wouldn't miss it."

Then Johnson appeared, navy suit, red and white striped tie – all business.

"Max! Buddy." He swept an arm towards his office. "Come on in."

Max shot Mandy a parting grin and disappeared into the office behind Johnson.

"So we have your signing arranged for Saturday next at the Queens Park in your home town." He turned to face Max.

Max looked stunned. "You have?"

The publisher looked at him and frowned. "You knew we were arranging it."

"Well, yes of course." He lifted a toe and rested it on the rubber of his thong. "But it just seems so real now."

Johnson slapped him on the shoulder. "Don't worry about it buddy. You'll do fine." He raised an eyebrow. "I have faith in you." Then he cast a doubtful eye over Max's attire, sighed and blew out a breath. "Although, we do have a couple of details to go over."

Max frowned.

The publisher ignored it. "Why don't we get some lunch and then we can talk turkey."

Always with the turkey.

Max piped up. "I'll go get it." *Anything to get out of this stuffy office.*

The publisher's eyes grew wide. "Game to explore the city hey?"

You're an idiot Johnson.

"Well listen, get Mandy to give you a mud map to this great café near the river. They make the best focaccias."

Fuck…who?

Mandy looked up in surprise as Max walked out. "Finished already?"

He shook his head. "Nope. Just going out to grab some lunch. Johnno said you'd be able to give me a map to get some fuckers." *Close enough.*

Mandy peeled out a girlie laugh, then pretended to wipe a tear away from her eye. "Oh Max, you really are too much." Then a thought struck her in that juvenile way. "Can you get me some lunch too?"

He shrugged. "Sure. Just write it down." Then he added. "And don't forget the map."

Mandy pointed a pencil at him. "You know. They have great focaccias at the café in the lobby of the building just on the river – do you know it?"

Thought we covered that already. "Nope. But I'm gonna hope that's some sort of sandwich."

She giggled as she scribbled out a quick idiot's map and directions – and the list of food they wanted. She handed it to Max. "It's a bit of a hike." Then a second thought later. "But not that far really – for you."

"Thanks." He took it, looked at it. "Send out a search party if I'm not back by two o'clock."

She laughed at him. And as she watched him walk through the glass doors, a thought crossed her mind – *I wonder if they have a dress code for that café?*

Max retraced his steps, and stepped back out into the mall. He followed Mandy's mud map for a few very busy streets until he saw the building up ahead. *And the river.* He hadn't been down to this part of town before. *Swish.*

He headed towards the point at the building where Mandy had written an 'X' marks the spot on her map.

That must be it. He looked up at the massive, polished steel columns in the foyer. *Wow!* This was some building. It's glass and steel revolving door entrance was massive and very impressive. He stepped into the revolving glass panels, hated the momentary feeling of being trapped, then breathed a quick sigh of relief when the doors spat him out on the inside of the building.

He was immediately in a great expanse of granite – floor tiles, walls – everywhere he looked was gloss, gloss and gloss. He took in the surrounds, he'd never seen anything like it.

He shot a quick glance around, got his bearings, then started to cross the vast lobby, his thongs clacking across the granite tiles and headed towards the sign that said "The Bean n' Stalk" café. So far Mandy's instructions were spot on. *She'd obviously been here before.*

He cocked his head and listened. *Was that a piano playing?*

He spied the café counter, and sauntered up, taking his place in the cue. The line moved down quickly but Max was completely distracted by the full length view of the river outside. The illusion was that the building was sitting in the water, and he guessed it was all a treat for city folk who didn't see the water very often.

He stretched his gaze out into the distance. He noticed motorboats tied up at wharfs. He noticed people trailing down the jetties towards the boats.

But what he failed to notice, was the dark haired, green-eyed woman in the grey suit, huddled over a file spread out on a table in a makeshift work booth.

He took his turn in the line and stepped up to the blonde waitress at the counter – check that, her badge said "Manager".

"Can I help you?" She asked as anonymously as she did to every other person that walked up to her counter.

Max held out Mandy's note with the description of the food he wanted. He wasn't even going to try to say it.

The blonde manager smiled as she reached out a hand and took the paper. Then she absently lifted her eyes up to meet her customer's. A shot of electricity bolted through her. She stepped back, smile vanished.

"Is something wrong?" Max asked.

"No…no of course not." She tried to cover, unconvincingly. "It's just that we don't see this order very often – it was just a surprise that's all." *Stupid stupid.*

Max squinted at her in disbelief. "Uh huh." *City folk.*

"Ok, let's check your order." She stepped forward with his piece of paper – started scribbling on an order pad – she was all business again.

Max cocked his head, his eyes narrowed. *Did she look familiar?* "Do I know you from somewhere."

The guy in the line behind Max snickered.

"I doubt it." The manager snapped off a response. Then she spun around to pass his order through to the servery.

"If you'd like to wait over there sir." She pointed away from the tables and booths.

He nodded at her – while the cogs turned slowly – too slowly. He knew her from somewhere – *but where? No.* He shook it off. *Probably just imagining it. Everyone looks the same in the city.* He followed her directions and stood off to the side.

His order was up quick smart. She called his number.

He raised his eyebrows. "That was quick."

She handed him his order, then made a show of fussing with something under the counter.

Max felt the warmth from the paper bag. It smelled good too. Mandy was right. He turned to go, but something still niggled him. He looked directly into the manager's eyes. "It's just that you seem familiar."

"I get that a lot." She smiled insincerely and glanced away. "Come's with the territory. You have a nice day sir." *Get out of here.* She motioned for the next customer.

Max shook his head, smiled and let it go. "You too." But she seemed to have stopped listening.

He backtracked over the expansive lobby and marched towards the revolving door. His stomach growled. Hunger steamrolled in, flattening any new thoughts.

He was barely out of the building, before he'd forgotten all about the familiar blonde manager at The Bean n' Stalk cafe.

Chapter Fifteen

Max leaped out of bed the instant his eyes were open. He showered quickly and donned the designated clothes for the day. Then clomped down the hallway and into his kitchen.

He flicked on the kettle, grabbed a bowl, the box of all-bran, some fruit, milk and honey. He heaped the fruit and honey onto the cereal in the bowl, wrenched open the drawer under the little island bench, grabbed a spoon, plonked down on a stool and started scooping the mixture into his mouth. His foot found the bottom rail of the stool, his leg twitching out of control.

He closed his eyes as he chewed. *Book signing day.* His foot bounced harder on the rail.

The shrill tones of the Bohemian Rhapsody suddenly punctured his quiet. *His phone.* He raced back down the hall to his bedroom and picked it up before it stopped ringing. He glanced at the caller id. *'Randolf Johnson."*

"Johnno. What's up?"

"Just checking on you buddy. You ready for

today?"

Johnson had lined up the book signing to be held in the rotunda in Queens Park – the main park in town. "Good enough for Kylie Minogue," he'd said. "Good enough for Max Martin." That was true enough – the Kylie Minogue part that is – the rotunda had been used in one of her early movies. Big thing in the town at the time.

Johnson chose a Saturday for Max's book debut. Small town. Who wouldn't want to go to a good erotica book event on the weekend? "It'll draw the crowds," he'd said.

Only one thought from that statement had resonated in Max's head – *there's going to be crowds?*

"Romantic setting." Johnson had told him, although that was probably Mandy's digging that uncovered that little nugget.

"Max! You there?"

Max nodded into the phone. "Yeah yeah."

"You're not nervous are you buddy?"

Maybe a little.

But Johnson kept yabbering. "Listen, we'll set you up in the rotunda, not far from the big cannons near the river. They're going to make great phallic symbols."

"Great what?" Max frowned. *Jesus – as if it wasn't embarrassing enough already.*

Johnson ignored him. "It is an erotica book after all. We can afford to be a bit cheeky."

Max heard the glee in the publisher's voice. *You're a woman Johnson.*

"You got the clothes I sent you?"

He cringed. "Yeah I got 'em." Johnson had fitted him for a suit the last time he was in the city.

Max ran a hand through the lame arse, blue tie hanging around his neck. "Look is this really necessary? It's not really me."

His publisher's voice tightened. "It may not be you Max, but it is us. We've got a lot invested here." *All business again.*

"Fair enough."

A rapid knock at the door startled him. *Had to be Baldo.*

"Come in, it's open!" He yelled, not bothering to hold the phone away. "Gotta go Johnno. See you at the park later."

"Wai…."

Max hit the end button.

He glanced down the hallway and watched his mate breeze in.

Gary took one look at Max and stopped dead in his tracks. He sucked in his lips trying to stifle a smirk. "Nice suit."

"Shut up Baldo." Max pouted as he glared down at the long white, crisp shirt sleeves. "Now I know how a penguin feels."

"Now we can both go work at Seaworld hey?" He tried – although not really that hard – to hold it in, but the laughter rocketed out of him. *Good to get a bit of his own back.* He ran a hand down the front of his own pastel coloured shirt. "Glad I got to pick out my own suit."

Max frowned at him. "Is your suit pink?"

"No." He snapped, the funny all gone.

"It is. It's pink."

"It's not pink."

Max sighed. His face slumped. Another retort wasn't in him this morning. Even teasing Baldo didn't hold the same appeal. He rubbed a hand over the stupid sleeves.

"Mate, seriously you look fine. Just not used to seeing you in a suit. Stop worrying." Then he spotted the mess Max had made of his tie. "Come here."

"What?" Max reared back and glared at him like a red belly black preparing to strike.

Gary held up his hands. "Just wanna fix your tie. Don't flatter yourself."

Max took a reluctant step towards him, and let him fuss with his tie. "This is weird."

"Hold still." Gary flipped and tucked and within seconds Max had a perfectly bound neck tie.

He checked it out in the hall mirror. "Not bad. You're going to make someone a great wife one day mate." *Ok, that felt a little better.*

"Yeah? Well I'm not the one standing there in the pretty suit and tie."

He scowled. "Johnson says I have to wear it."

Gary jiggled his keys, his voice meant business. "You ready?"

Max held up a finger. "Not quite." He raced into the bathroom, brushed his teeth, swept a hand through his sandy hair and admired his neatly trimmed, now almost non-existent goatee. He then squirted on some ridiculous fragrance from a small, glass bottle that Johnson had sent along with the suit and demanded that he use it. *"Attracts the ladies,"* Johnson had said.

Then he shoved on the matching jacket, grabbed his wallet and keys, then hightailed it back to the hallway.

He blew out a deep breath. "Ready as I'll ever be." Then in a rare moment of gratitude he felt compelled to say, "Thanks for coming today mate."

Baldo smiled at him. "Mate, I wouldn't miss this for the world."

***

Max pulled his Colorado truck into a bitumen carpark at the street side of Queens Park. He cut the engine, but remained in the truck. *What had he gotten himself into? He couldn't do this.*

He cast his eyes out over the grounds directly ahead. A few people were milling. *Not sure if they're here for the book event.* The park was familiar, but it had also changed. He hadn't been here in a while – probably not since he was a teenager up to no good. He cringed at the thought. It felt weird being back here as an adult doing something legitimate. *If you could call what he was about to do today legitimate.*

But he had to admit, the park was a beautiful spot. It was a grand, old park located in an old part of town – very old – eighteen hundreds old. The park was a sprawling and elegant piece of local history – *probably heritage listed.* Its lush green grass, fernery, mini waterfall and exquisite gardens were immaculately maintained. He squinted into the distance, just able to make out a floral archway over the footpath. *When did they build that?*

Max could easily see why Johnson had insisted on holding the book event here. Of course it helped that the author of Mary Poppins was born in the building around the corner. A source of pride for the locals – who celebrated that fact every year with a Mary Poppins festival. It was a blast from the past, gaining popularity and catching the world's attention – on occasion.

The park sat alongside its namesake – the Mary River – which had not always treated it so kindly. It had gone under water courtesy of the Mary more times than Max could count over the past few years.

"Look." Gary tapped the window and pointed towards the band rotunda. It was decked out with a couple of tables, a few chairs, piles of books, *and was that an enlarged poster of Max's face hanging from the lacework?*

Gary's eyes lit up like Christmas balls. "Max!"

Max jumped in his seat. Snapped out of his trance.

"Jesus Baldo. Cat on a hot tin roof here."

"Sorry." He grinned. "And that's my expression by the way. You never finished reading it in high school remember? And anyway, you can't just use my expressions."

Max shook his head with wide eyes. "I never did a lot of things in high school I should have." He smirked. "Anyway it wasn't on the curriculum Baldo, you frickin' goody two shoes. And besides, you don't own the expression."

Gary straightened in the passenger seat. *Ok, enough procrastination.* The numbers were starting to swell as the start time approached. A definite group was congregating around the rotunda.

Max sank in his seat. "Jesus, haven't they got anything else to do in this town?"

His mate smiled. "Probably just excited to see the town's new star." He let out a quick laugh. "Besides, didn't you say the publishers have been promoting this like crazy?"

He could only stare in disbelief. *What had he gotten himself into?* "But I'm just signing a few books. It's not that big a deal. This is embarrassing."

His mate frowned. "Yeah, but this is your hometown Max. People are interested."

He grunted. He hated crowds, reminded him of the city – and knowing that a lot of people in the crowd today would probably know him personally, didn't help.

He wriggled in the car seat. "Yeah well I don't really want the interest. I just wanted to pay my mortgage remember?" It came out as a whine.

Max flicked his eyes back out over the crowd. He already recognised a few people. But there was one he wasn't expecting. *Frank* – his old boss. He squinted to see past Frank and then two more familiar figures sprang up – *Rob and Kyle.*

Frank looked up at the truck and waved.

Max sank further into the seat. "Fuck I can't do this Baldo."

"Yes you can. Look Frank's trying to tell you something."

His former boss mouthed some words.

"I can't tell what he's saying from here."

Gary grinned. "I think he said good luck."

"That's it. I'm out of here." He turned the key in the ignition and the truck roared to life again. He glanced over his shoulder to pull out, but – he wasn't going anywhere. A horn blasted beside them. They glimpsed the driver.

Johnson! Fuck!

Then the little car's horn tooted again.

Max and Gary exchanged looks. *City folk.*

"Hi Max." Johnson rolled down his window, his tone brisk and rushed. He'd been to the park already this morning to supervise setting up.

Max sighed and switched off his engine again. "Hey."

Johnson beamed up at him. "All ready?" It wasn't really a question. More like an expectation – or a hope.

"Sure." Max was resigned to his fate.

"Hi Max." A female voice called out from Johnson's passenger seat. "Ready for your big day?" She vibrated with excitement.

Max smiled at her, but his voice was strained. "Hey Mandy." He wished he could share her enthusiasm.

He groaned a little on the inside. Then dutifully introduced his mate to Mandy and Johnson.

Mandy's eyes were suddenly childlike. "Baldo! I've heard so much about you."

Gary raised his eyebrows at Max. *Is that right?* Then he returned her smile. "I hope it was all good."

Max shook his head and pushed open his door. "Come on then. Let's get this over with."

The foursome ambled down towards the crowds.

Mandy breathed in the gloriously cool winter morning. *Perfect. Fresh.*

Max fidgeted with his tie. *At least he wouldn't get hot and sweaty today – thank god it's Winter.* But he still felt like a prized peacock. He ripped off the tie. *Better.*

Gary grinned.

Johnson frowned.

They headed towards the rotunda – an exquisite, piece of local history painted maroon, green, and cream. An ornament sat atop, which Max always liked to think of as a mini bell-tower.

Park seats were positioned in rows at the front – an automatic audience for when bands actually played here.

Max caught his breath. *Wow becoming real now.* Then he frowned at a sudden thought. "Who's minding the store?"

His publisher attempted to hide an uneasy look. "Ah…we left an assistant in charge till we got back." He exchanged a nervous glance with Mandy.

Max and Gary caught the exchange and swapped suspicious looks of their own. *What's that about?*

Then as they drew nearer, the full spectacle in the rotunda came into view.

Max nearly choked. "Jesus! What the fuck is that?" He pointed to a huge picture of his own face staring back at him.

Johnson blurted out a surprised laugh. "Well what did you think we were going to put up?"

"You said 'picture'. You didn't say anything about hangin' a town banner!"

He chuckled, ignoring Max's angst. He'd gotten used to his tantrums. "All part of it mate." He winked.

Gary shoved in front of Max. "It all looks great." He enthused, ignoring Max's icy glare. "Wow. Look at all your books Max." He pointed to the table stacked with Max's book.

Max eyed off the table. *Wow, it did look good.* A small thrill ran through him – a flutter of excitement even. He had to admit, it *was* something to see the finished product.

Gary turned to Mandy. "What are the extra chairs for?"

She smiled. "If Max has time, some readers might like to sit and chat with him."

Max flung his head around. "What?"

Johnson raised a hand to settle him. "People like to ask questions. You know, why did you write the book? Where did you get the ideas for your characters? That sort of thing."

Max groaned. He hoped it was busy and people moved on quickly.

"Couldn't you have just put a sign up Johnno?" Max rolled his eyes. "I don't want to be fuckin' repeatin' myself all day."

His voice raised eyebrows and turned heads. Then one crowd member glanced over.

"It's Max!" An excited woman called out to her friend, a copy of the book in her hand.

"God, how embarrassing." Max whispered to his mate, his voice pleading – *get me out of here!*

Right that's it! Gary snapped his head around. His mouth moved, but his teeth remained together. "Talk about ungrateful. It's all part of it Max. What did ya think was gonna happen when you started this?" Then he waved and smiled to the woman on Max's behalf, as if nothing was wrong.

"Not this." Max hissed. "I just wanted to pay my mortgage."

Gary's voice was surprisingly stern. "Jesus Max, embrace something for once in your life. This is a great opportunity, so stop your bitchin'."

Max's eyes widened, then a broad grin spread across his face. *Baldo's got a backbone after all.* "Ok, keep your knickers on Baldo."

Then they both bellowed out a laugh at the same time at the irony.

Johnson leaned in towards them. "Jesus. Will you both behave?" He rolled his eyes at Mandy. *Country folk.*

The foursome stepped up into the rotunda.

Gary glanced around for the assistant, but he couldn't see anyone that resembled what he expected an assistant would look like.

Mandy settled the star attraction into his seat – and made sure Baldo was close by – *for support.*

Her boss watched on impressed. Mandy had a real way with Max. For some reason, he didn't fight the system so much when it was her dishing out the orders.

The line of people wanting a book signed or to just talk to Max, formed instantly. It took on a life of its own – moving, swaying, shortening, lengthening. After a while, it didn't look like a line of people – it just looked like a line.

The first woman to step up gushed at Max. "Sign my book Max."

"Ah, sure." He scribbled something benign in the cover of her copy.

She seemed to love it. She held the book up to her chest, winked at Max and shot him a suggestive look – which left nothing to the imagination. "I'll treasure it."

Max faked a smile. "You do that love."

Gary pouted at him and pointed a scolding finger in the air. His message clear – *be nice.*

A couple dozen scribbles later, Max's hand was getting sore. He glanced up at the line, still a few to go. *This wasn't so bad.*

Then suddenly Frank materialised next in line. And as Max looked up at his former boss, a flash went off in his face – a local photographer had snapped a picture – making sure Frank was in it.

Max rolled his eyes. "That going on the window of The Outboard Shop Frankie?"

Frank gave him a cheeky smirk, and held out a copy of the book. "No hard feelings mate?" Then he cleared his throat as if he was about to deliver a rehearsed line. "For the missus." His eyes indicated the book.

Uh-huh. Max grabbed the book and grinned up at his old boss. He scratched out a message, then handed it back to him. "No hard feelings mate."

Frank opened the cover and read the inside jacket. It read: *'Can I have my job back you prick? Max Martin.'* He read it again and laughed out loud. "Yeah mate. If that's what you really want. I reckon it'd be a bit hard to convince anyone that you got something against women now. How's next Monday suit?"

"Suits me just fine." He smiled.

Max spent a good hour signing, scribbling and explaining his existence and what possessed him to write the book. He started out with grand explanations. "Had a vision," "wanted to say something important about the differences between men and women." Then he became a robot. "Needed the money," "had to pay my mortgage." People giggled at those – *"what a kidder that Max Martin is."*

Almost another full hour later and he was nearly finished – besides he had to take a leak soon or he'd burst. He glanced up – three left in the cue.

Johnson hovered by Max's side, fussing with the few copies of the book left on the table. He raised his eyebrows – *they'd actually sold quite a few.*

Apparently that was a good sign because as Johnson had told them, books don't always sell at signings.

"Then why am I doin' it?" Max had asked.

"To connect with your readers."

The last woman in the cue stepped forward. She wore an emerald green soft, woollen sweater and blue jeans, hair pulled up in a ponytail.

Max looked up with the dull expression he'd perfected over the past couple of hours.

Then he froze.

He was instantly still – except for his heart. He felt his heartbeat lurch to full throttle, as he looked up into the face of the woman in green.

She smiled at him. Her voice soft. "Hello Max."

Did his heart just leap into his throat? He barely whispered the word that was fighting its way down his tongue. "Kat."

Her smile broadened.

Max slowly rose to his feet. "It's you."

She nodded. "It's good to see you Max." Her voice wavered ever so slightly.

He stared in disbelief. "It's really you." Then his brow furrowed as he came back to Earth with a thud.

"I don't understand…how did you know I was here?"

She winked at Johnson. "A little bird told me."

Max's expression was puzzled. He shook his head. "I don't understand."

Johnson stepped forward. *Time to fess up.* "Max." He said quietly. "This is your ghostwriter."

Ghostwriter? He glanced at her, mouth open. "What?"

Then he shot a look back at his publisher. "How?"

Kat spoke first. "I'm a ghostwriter Max. That's what I do."

Max thought hard. *No, he definitely didn't recall her telling him that before — or much at all about her job the night they'd met, come to think of it.* She'd danced around the topic of work. Then distracted him with a lot of questions about his own work.

Johnson stepped in to offer further explanation. "Katherine sent a proposal to me the night she met you. She emailed the proposal and the changes she made to your work – on your behalf of course."

Max glanced at Kat. His eyes still wide – the surprise compounding.

Gary stood back, watching and listening.

Johnson continued. "She's worked for us before, ghostwriting on a number of projects. When she told me she would get on board with you, I knew she'd be able to work miracles with you." He grinned. "You've got her to thank. She's the one who really believed in you…and your ideas."

Max huffed. *Well that explains it.* Then he frowned. "You're a prick you know that Johnson?"

"Yeah I know."

Then he huffed again, more than a little bit irritated. "Why didn't you tell me? I asked you about her." *God did he sound like a brat?*

Johnson put his hand on his heart. "I wanted to Max, but I couldn't tell you."

"Why not?" He felt his anger rise – and it wasn't just directed at his publisher. He checked himself. *What was he doing? Why was he doing this?* He was letting the embarrassment he felt over their deception, consume him.

But all he really wanted to do was grab hold of the woman who stole his heart all those months ago – the woman who was standing in front of him now – and pull her towards him, and hold onto her and never let her go.

Johnson continued. "Well for one, I didn't want you distracted-"

"Distracted!" Max cut him off. He thought about hitting him, then remembered where he was.

Gary stepped up. "Lower your voice Max."

Kat jumped to Johnson's defence. Her voice calm – the voice of reason. "It was me Max." She looked him directly in the eyes, forcing him to look at her. "I swore him to secrecy. I told him I wouldn't work on the project if you knew."

"But why?" His voice strangled by confusion.

"I wanted to keep things professional. I wanted you to be able to write to an anonymous person."

Her heart sank at his pained expression. She took a step towards him.

He could smell her perfume – soft, delicate. He felt his heart beat faster as she moved closer to him. It beat so hard he thought it might actually burst.

She smiled at him.

That smile – God it's really her.

Her voice sweet, caring. "I thought I could draw out your best, unaffected work – give you the space to grow as a writer without having to try and impress me…or anybody else." She quickly added that last part. "Randy and I go way back. He agreed to my terms."

Randy?

She lowered her eyes. "When I first read your work, I admit, I thought it…needed work." She raised her eyes to meet his. She wanted to reach out and touch him – to reassure him. "But I'd met you, talked to you, and I saw something in you. I just wanted you to focus on bringing out who you are in your writing – without any distractions."

She felt the heat in her cheeks. *Was she being too presumptuous?* It was only one night. Then as if she needed to sum up her deception. "I did it for you Max. I wanted it for you." *Had she waited too long?*

Max watched her face. Listened to what she was saying. He saw the same coy expression he'd seen so many months ago. His heart pounded out of his chest. He was certain of her sincerity. *Of course she was telling the truth.* This was his Kat.

A flicker of happiness ignited inside him. Doubts vanquished. Soul-crushing disappointment cast out to distant memory. His anger melted away – like a tiny ice flake too close to the flame. The flicker suddenly burst into a raging fire.

Of course he understood – *when she put it that way.*

Truthfully, she had him, hook line and sinker, the moment she stepped towards him. Every word since then was just reeling him in. There was nothing left to do but reach out for her and-

Why was he hesitating? Why was he not reaching for her? Idiot Max.

She chuckled at him.

The sound of her laugh.

She took another step towards him. Stopped and smiled. "You smell good Max."

That was it. He grabbed her and pulled her into him.

She laughed out loud, surprised and excited at the same time, once again oblivious to everything else around them.

He stroked her hair. "You smell good too." Then in sudden move he'd once seen in a movie – and had scoffed at it at the time – he hoisted her high in the air above him, then slid her body slowly back down the length of his own.

She sighed at the feeling and marvelled at his strength. *Like a feather.*

Then he lowered her down until their faces met again. "Kat." He whispered. "I've missed you."

She smiled, but it was her eyes that told him. "I've missed you too."

Then he closed the gap between them, bringing his lips gently down onto hers and held her in a soft embrace.

Bursts of loud applause erupted around them, punctuated by loud hoots and whistles – mainly from the few men in the crowd. It snagged them back to reality. And they remembered where they were. Didn't care.

Max wrapped his arms around his woman and hugged her tight – he never wanted to let her go again. Then he drew her back to look at him. "I'm so happy to see you."

They laughed as they heard more random call outs from the crowd.

"So romantic," someone gushed.

"Aww, look at them."

Then the surprising, "Go for it Max!"

Max cocked an eyebrow and Kat laughed out loud again, long and free.

Gary stepped up towards them. Cleared his throat.

"Baldo!" Max ushered him closer. "Meet Kat." He announced her name like it was the most important word in the world.

Baldo placed his hands over hers in a warm welcome. "Kat. It's my absolute pleasure. I've heard a lot about you."

Max frowned. "Hands off Baldo." Then he laughed at his mate – *just kidding*. Then he frowned again. "Seriously Baldo, get your hands off her-"

He was cut off by a sudden, urgent flurry of activity nearby. A shrill female voice called out – its owner stumbled up the steps of the rotunda, she tripped and sprawled out an awkward mess on the rotunda floor.

The woman cried out as her bag vaulted ahead of her, spewing out its contents in front of them all.

"Oh no!" She squealed out.

Gary rushed over to help her. "Are you ok?" He held out a hand. "Here, let me help you up."

She accepted his hand with a grateful smile, eyelashes flapping, and managed to scramble to her feet.

Gary swung into action again. He dived down and gathered up the wayward items, quickly returning them to her bag, then returned the bag to its owner – *its beautiful, sexy, breathtaking owner.*

Her appreciation weaved through her melodic tones. "Oh, thank you so much," she said without looking at him, her focus shot down to her legs. "Oh no." She inspected the damage to her stockings. *Shouldn't have worn the mini skirt.*

She straightened up and ran her hands down her sides to her hips, smoothing out the conservative, pink sweater – that Kat had made her wear – but she couldn't hide the buxom bosoms.

An unruly blonde curl drifted across her eye. She flicked it back into place completely distracted by her own state of affairs. "Oh look at me, I'm all dirty now." She dusted herself off. Then glanced up, wide-eyed to see her friend smiling back at her. "Oh Kat, I'm so sorry I'm la-"

She stopped talking. Her eyes shifted, connecting with those of possibly the most gorgeous man she'd ever seen.

Gary returned her gaze, his voice gentle. "You look fine." He assured her.

Kat frowned, but was very much amused by the events unfolding in front her. "Sal? Are you ok?"

"Uh huh." But Sally couldn't tear her eyes away.

Max shot a glance at his mate. Then back to the woman in pink. Then back again to Baldo.

Unbelievable! Two strangers equally smitten – equally immobile. He erupted with a loud, riotous laugh.

Kat turned to Max. "Max, you remember Sal?"

That stopped him – as good as if she'd slapped him.

"Sal?" *Right that was her name.* He smacked his forehead with his hand as the memory flooded back. Then he stepped forward to meet her, stopping suddenly when it dawned on him that he already had.

He eyed the blonde Sally in front of him. Then another lightning bolt struck. "Hey!" He bounced a finger in the air at Sally. "You're the manager from that café."

Sal flashed a reluctant look at Max. "Guilty. Sorry Max. I was sworn to secrecy." Then she babbled. "I nearly died that day when you walked into my café. I felt so sorry for you. I almost made Kat confess everything to you right there on the spot-"

"Sal." Kat interrupted. She pointed to the man standing in front of her friend.

Sally blushed. "Oh."

"This is Max's friend Baldo."

Her heart raced. Her tone soft again. "Baldo?"

Baldo lifted up her hand and kissed the back of it. "It's Gary actually. Everyone just calls me Baldo."

Max burst out another hearty laugh. *Baldo you're still a pussy.*

Sal smiled then wiggled an eyebrow at Kat like a cheeky schoolgirl. "He seems nice." She whispered – but everyone heard.

Katherine frowned at her, but her tone was forgiving. "I thought you said 'nice' was boring."

Sally snickered out a fake giggle. Then with wide

eyes and a haughty pout, she said, "Well, isn't it a woman's prerogative to change her mind?"

Chapter Sixteen

In a small town, far away from Brisbane city, Max Martin put the key in the lock of his solid timber front door.

He turned the key and gently pushed the door wide open until he heard it tap against the wall inside.

It was another Saturday night, and it had been two months since his book release. Life was getting back to normal – almost.

He'd picked up a really hot chick at the local RSL tonight and he was bringing her home. *She was a sure thing tonight.*

He reached an arm through the doorway, and stretched around to touch the light switch on the wall.

He flicked the switch. Instantly, light spilled out of the doorway and onto Max, illuminating the shimmering fleck in his smart, navy suit – no tie.

His hair was washed and neatly combed. He had showered at least once that day and planned on doing it again that night. And he'd used that ridiculous bottle of fragrance again.

He turned and checked on his female companion behind him. He was determined to be attentive tonight.

In a sudden burst of spontaneity, he swept the woman off her feet and carried her over the threshold and into the house, kicking the door shut behind him.

She peeled out a squeal of delight, the massive skirt on her gown rustled, the layers of tulle underneath swished up, exposing her white, strappy heels.

"Mrs Martin," he said, mimicking a posh voice.

Kat giggled her response. "Mr Martin."

Max carried his new bride down the corridor and towards the bedroom.

She squealed again with excitement, pretending to kick all the way down the hall. They'd had so much fun at their reception tonight. *Max was right*. The RSL was the best reception centre in town.

He placed her down gently on the bed – which he just then noticed was suffocating from a layer of rose petals, flowers and was that…*potpourri?*

Baldo!

Max snorted. "That pussy." He smiled at Kat. "I really do need to get those keys back."

She laughed at him, her eyes glistened. Something told her Sal might also have had a hand in it. She breathed in the sweet perfume, enchanted by the array of coloured flowers. "How wonderful."

"Yeah he's wonderful." But Max had other things on his mind.

He made short work of getting her out of her gown and under the covers.

Then he pounced over the top of her, like a big cat

over its prey – his eyes betraying his intent. "Is getting married enough foreplay for you Mrs Martin?"

She flung her head back against the pillows and laughed, her dark hair flowing free over her exposed shoulders. "What do you think?"

Max reached a hand around her head, leaned down and kissed her softly on the forehead.

God she felt happy. Her smile was immovable. Everything finally fit.

She looked into his gorgeous, green eyes and asked him seriously. "How is it that you ended up being my type of man?"

Max smirked. "Because I know what women really want." He wiggled an eyebrow at her. "And it's me baby."

She laughed out loud. "Give it up Max." She didn't need convincing. He already had her heart.

Her laugh trickled to a stop. She breathed out a tender sigh and looked directly up into his eyes. "Seriously, I feel like I really know you Max." She smiled again, her eyes cheeky. "I had an insight remember? From reading your work."

"Well Mrs Martin. I feel like I know you too from reading my work." He smirked. *Ghostwriter.*

Her eyes flew wide open with mock surprise. "That's right."

He returned her gaze. "But I think I got the better end of the deal. Because thanks to you, I think I'm going to do very well tonight." He had a twinkle in his eye – then he winked. "Because I got a hot tip."

She giggled and pulled him down onto her. "Well Max Martin, I hope you know what to do with that."

Then she pulled the super soft blanket up over them
and pulled Max deep down under it.